WHACKED

A RYLIE COOPER MYSTERY

STELLA BIXBY

FERRY TAIL PUBLISHING LLC

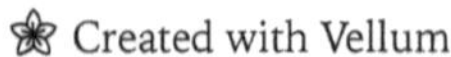 Created with Vellum

For Grant. I'm so thankful I'm your mommy.

Garrett raised his sword with the fluidity of a trained knight.

His opponent—my nephew—was a quarter of his size, yet with only slightly less skill.

Concentration hardened their features.

I laughed.

Garrett was undeniably gorgeous. Tall and fit—you would never guess he was an accountant by trade. My nephew, all grit and determination, stared up at Garrett undeterred by the difference in stature.

The little boy swiped his sword down at an angle, catching Garrett's shins and bringing him to his knees in faux-defeat.

"You got me." Garrett fell to the warm sand. "I wasn't quick enough."

My nephew jumped up and yelled, "Hooray!"

"Not so fast." I swiped the foam sword from a groaning Garrett. "You haven't defeated me."

"Princesses can't wield swords," my nephew cried out.

"Princesses can do anything," I said. "But I am no princess."

"You can say that again," my mother muttered from the picnic blanket where she sat next to my father and my other nephews.

I didn't have time to roll my eyes. My nephew was going in for the kill. His foam sword slashed through the air, only to meet the squishiness of my own, saving my ankles from the blow

We battled for at least a minute, our swords meeting above and below our heads.

"Not bad for a princess," my nephew said between breaths.

"I said, I wasn't a princess." I took one last swing and brought the foam blade across his calf.

He did a perfect impersonation of what Garrett had done and fell to the ground in a glorious display of agony.

"I'm dying. I'm dying." His voice weakened as he fell. "I'm dead." He came to rest next to Garrett, his arms splayed out, his tongue falling from his mouth to his cheek.

I laughed and held out a hand to help him up, but my nephew swung a leg out, catching me in the back of my knees, and causing me to fall forward into the sand.

He reached for my sword, but I was too quick. I slashed it across his stomach.

He fell to the ground again, twitching in fake agony.

"I am the victor." I jumped up and raised my sword above my head.

"You beat an eight-year-old," my mom said.

"And a mighty challenger at that," Garrett said. "Let's see if I can revive him."

Before my nephew realized what was coming, Garrett was tickling his sides.

I plopped down and joined him in the tickle-fest.

"Okay, okay," my nephew said through giggles. "I'm alive."

We stopped and laughed.

"Why don't the three of you get over here and have some lunch," Mom said. "I made chicken salad sandwiches with grapes."

My nephew jumped up and rushed to the picnic basket.

"My future wife is pretty good with a sword." Garrett rolled onto his side to kiss me.

Sand crept up my shorts, but it was worth it.

"Ewwww," my nephew said.

"I've had a lot of practice." I laughed. "We better eat before my mom loses her mind."

"Your mom loves me," Garrett said.

"How could she not? You're so lovable." I kissed him again.

For the past couple of months, Garrett and I had been on cloud nine. Work had been dead quiet—no bodies, buried appendages, or missing persons—which kept the stress down for both of us.

"Hey, this is a public park. There are kids around," Ben—one of my co-workers and a park ranger at the Alder Ridge Reservoir—said with a smile.

"There are?" I raised onto my elbows and looked around. "I had no idea."

Normally, I didn't spend my time off where I worked. But there was no denying the reservoir was one of the most pristine parks in the Denver metro area and the perfect place for a picnic with the family. The white sand beach—not natural, of course—was the cleanest I'd ever set foot on, and the kids loved building sandcastles when they weren't swimming or playing on the playground.

"Would you like a sandwich?" My mom offered Ben.

"No, thank you." Ben wiped a hand over his forehead before replacing his ballcap. "The guys and I are having a grill-off today. Feel free to come join in the fun."

"Maybe we will," I said as Garrett helped me up to a stand. "Am I working with you tomorrow?"

I brushed sand from my legs.

"Tomorrow?" Ben looked out at the water. "Uh, no."

I looked up at him. "But I thought that's what the schedule—"

"The summies start tomorrow." The words fell out of Ben's mouth, and an apologetic look washed over his face.

"Tomorrow?" I asked. "Why isn't that on the schedule?"

"Ursula moved up their start date."

"But shouldn't they do their classroom time first? I don't have to be there for that, do I?"

Ben shrugged.

"Why is this a bad thing?" Garrett asked.

"Remember?" I said. "I told you I was going to be in charge of training Ursula's niece?"

"Oh, right? Gira—"

"Victoria," I interrupted Garrett. "Her name is Victoria, right?" I looked at Ben, who didn't seem to notice me completely interrupting Garrett.

"I think so." Ben looked at me. "I'm sorry you're getting stuck with the boss's niece. Usually, the newbies don't get stuck training the summies."

"I'm not exactly a newbie," I said.

"You know what I mean," Ben said. "Someone who was a summie themselves the summer before."

"Most rangers don't go from being first-year summies to full-time rangers either," I teased.

"Yeah, yeah, you're amazing." Ben laughed. "If you need help with this one—" Ben said to Garrett "—let me know."

"I will," Garrett said. "Thanks."

"And get a room." He nudged me and winked at Garrett before walking back up the beach toward the offices.

"He doesn't know, does he?" Garrett asked.

"Doesn't know what?"

"That Victoria—or giraffe girl—is the reason your last relationship failed."

"No. He doesn't know," I said. "And he's not going to. She didn't seem to recognize me, so there's no reason to bring drama to a situation that doesn't warrant it."

My words were much more mature than my thoughts. I'd spent nearly every day thinking of ways to get out of training giraffe girl—the girl I'd found sleeping with my boyfriend of five years, and the reason I ended up as a park ranger for Prairie City, Colorado.

"Just don't let it get to you," Garrett said. "If she

hadn't slept with Troy, you wouldn't have ended up with me, right?"

I smiled up at him. "Right." It was nice that he was at least a head taller than me—few men were.

He bent down and kissed me quickly before looking around. "I don't think he saw."

We both burst out into laugher.

"I think we're safe," I said.

"Hey guys," another of my nephews—the oldest of the four—called out running over to us. "There's a crazy guy on the playground."

"As in a man?" I asked. "Or a kid?"

He shrugged. "Like a teenager, maybe? He's talking about a wolf-lady. I think he's high."

"How do you know about being high?" I asked.

"We have cable TV." He rolled his eyes dramatically.

"Take me to him," I said.

"Don't you think you should let Ben handle this?" Garrett said.

"I'm sure it's nothing," I said in my most calming voice. "Probably just some kid acting like an idiot."

But when I approached the playground, I knew it wasn't nothing.

And it definitely wasn't a teenager.

A grown man sat under the slide, talking to himself. And when I say talking, I mean yelling.

"She's not going to hurt you," he shouted. "Her wolf is tame."

He paused as if waiting for someone to answer, but the next voice was his.

"What if it's not tame? What if it attacks?"

I sucked in a breath. I did not need this on my day off. I should have listened to Garrett and called Ben back over. Even when I actively tried not to investigate situations, I ended up investigating anyway.

I shook my head. At least there weren't many kids on the playground.

"Hey." I peeked under the slide but kept a substantial distance in case the man tried to lunge out. "Are you okay?"

"Are you a cop?"

I glanced down at my cut-off jean shorts and white t-shirt and laughed. It had to be because of my aviator sunglasses. "Nope, just a park ranger. Off-duty, that is."

He looked to be in his mid-twenties, with blond dread-locks and torn clothes.

"Why don't you come out from under the slide?" I asked.

He didn't look at me but said, "The wolf lady will get us all."

This was beyond something I wanted to handle today. I took a few steps back, pulled out my phone, and texted Ben.

Crazy guy under the slide on the playground. Thinks a wolf lady is going to get us all. Can you take care of it?

Within seconds, Ben replied.

Be right there.

"Hey, bud," I said to my nephew. "Why don't you go back to the blanket with Grandma and Grandpa and Garrett?"

"But who'll protect you?" He looked up at me with his big brown eyes.

"This guy won't hurt anyone," I said. "Plus, I'm pretty tough."

"Not from him." He looked around. "From the wolf lady."

"I'm pretty sure there is no wolf lady," I said. "But I promise to be careful."

He hesitated before running back down to the beach.

The guy was still talking to himself, but now it was more of a whisper than a yell. Part of me wanted to question him. The other part of me knew I shouldn't get involved. Ben would handle it.

"Under the slide?" Ben asked, coming up beside me.

I nodded. "Do you know anything about a wolf lady?"

"I think I know what he's talking about," he said. "Nikki met with an author today whose books are about werewolves and vampires and that kind of stuff. She's holding her next book release party here. I guess when the author came to check out the reservoir, she brought a few —uh—characters with her."

"She brought a werewolf?"

"And a vampire." Ben shrugged. "I mean, they weren't real, of course—" He laughed at the thought "—but she needed them for her social media or something. Apparently, a good percentage of the people who come to the event will be in costume."

"Sounds . . . interesting."

"He probably saw the werewolf and got scared."

"I'm guessing he's high, so that probably didn't help."

"I'll take care of it. You get back to your family," Ben said. "And I'm really sorry to break the news about the schedule change."

"No worries," I said. "It's just one summer, how bad can it be?"

2

"Look what I got," Shayla said as she struggled to pull some sort of metal contraption through our apartment door the next morning.

"What is that?" Garrett asked. He'd stayed the night at my place and was currently sipping coffee and reading the newspaper.

"It's a stroller," Shayla said. "Well, actually a pram. But I think that's just a fancy name for stroller."

"Is there something you haven't told us?" I asked.

Shayla and I met when we were both summer park rangers. Now she's a police officer for the Prairie City Police Department and is dating one of the guys I work with.

Shayla's face turned bright red. "No. I'm not pregnant." She pushed her long wavy blonde hair out of her face and scowled at us.

"Then why buy a pram or stroller or whatever the heck that thing is?" I asked.

"Because I'm learning to rollerblade," she replied as if this explained everything.

"I can rollerblade," I said. "And I've never needed a stroller."

Shayla resumed trying to get the monstrosity inside the apartment. "Bella started rollerblading while pushing little Boyd in his stroller. She said it was really helpful with balance."

"So, you'll push an empty stroller while you rollerblade?"

Garrett was nearly bursting with laughter behind his newspaper.

Shayla finally got the stroller through the door, then reached back outside and pulled in a shopping bag.

"Not an empty stroller." She pulled a baby doll from the bag.

I couldn't keep it in any longer. I doubled over laughing. "You. Have. To. Be. Kidding." I managed between breaths. "Not so long ago, you were panicking about Seamus proposing, and now you're practicing to be a mom?"

Shayla looked like she might throw the baby doll at me. Garrett dropped the newspaper and laughed.

"I'm not practicing to be a mom," she said. "I'm trying to stay in shape."

"Maybe you should join them," Garrett said.

I gaped at him. "Are you saying I'm not in shape?"

He stopped laughing. "No! That's not—"

Shayla and I burst out laughing again.

Garrett looked relieved. "I just thought you could get a stroller too and practice for when we have our own baby."

I stopped laughing. That might have been worse than telling me I'm out of shape. "What do you mean, our own baby?"

"You want kids, right?"

He knew the answer. We had discussed children almost every day since we'd gotten engaged.

"Yes," I said. "Just not right now."

Shayla put a hand on my shoulder. "You're always welcome to join our rollerblading group." She giggled.

I stood. "Thanks for the invite." I shook my head and laughed. "I need to get ready for work."

<hr>

The entire drive to the reservoir, I dreaded working with Victoria. Even the top down, wind in my hair, brand new car feeling couldn't break me out of my funk. I never in a million years thought I'd get stuck training someone I despised.

"Good, everyone's here," Ursula said when I walked into the training room. "Please sit next to Victoria, Rylie."

I didn't realize we'd have such a formal sit-down opening to the training.

Victoria sat straight as a rod in her seat with a huge smile across her pretty face. Her bleach-blonde hair was up in the perfect ballerina bun, and her infamous long neck was accentuated by the deep V-neck t-shirt she wore.

I sat in the chair next to her, keeping as much distance as I could without looking suspicious. Even from a distance, I could smell her Hawaiian-punch-scented perfume.

She was smiling at me, but I kept my gaze straight ahead. I just needed to get this summer started so I could get it over with.

Ursula frowned at the two of us—probably mad we hadn't become instant-besties.

"I've worked with Greg." Ursula began her speech glancing over at Greg—the head ranger. "We've decided the trainees should spend a day with their training officers before they begin their classroom work."

Greg nodded along with every word Ursula said. None of the rangers crossed her. She was a tough cookie with a no-nonsense attitude.

"We think it will help you get to know one another and start the summer rangers off with a good impression of our beautiful park."

I glanced out the corner of my eye at the other newbies.

Nikki was paired up with a man who looked old enough to be her father. Ben sat next to a woman with half of her black hair shaved, and the other half in a long braid down her side. And Antonio sat next to another woman—probably in her mid-thirties—with brown hair and a stern look on her face.

"I'm incredibly excited about this year's summer rangers," Ursula continued. "Especially because, as you may know, my niece is one of them."

Victoria beamed next to me. I did my best not to roll my eyes. The only reason they hired Victoria was because she was related to Ursula.

"But I'll let her tell you about herself." Ursula motioned for Victoria to stand. "Why don't you begin, and then we'll go around the room so everyone can introduce themselves. Full-time rangers included."

"Thank you so much," Victoria began. "My name is Victoria Vilago. I recently graduated college with a degree in environmental engineering."

Okay, maybe they hired her for more than just being Ursula's niece.

Ugh.

Of course, she had to be smart.

"I'm excited to work with all of you," she continued. "Especially, you, Rylie."

My head shot up.

She was smiling down at me.

"I've heard so much about you from my aunt."

She pronounced aunt as if it rhymed with want.

I did my best to smile back at her. Was she messing with me? Surely, she had to remember the moment I walked in on her and my boyfriend—now ex-boyfriend—naked in my bed.

"Thank you, Victoria," Ursula said. "Rylie, how about you?"

I groaned internally but stood. "I'm Rylie. I was a summie—er—summer ranger—" It was common knowledge Ursula didn't like the term summie as it made the program sound unprofessional "—last summer and became a full-time ranger last fall. The past year has been rather exciting—"

"Shit magnet," Ben said through a fake cough behind me.

The other full-time rangers laughed.

Ursula cleared her throat, and the laughter stopped immediately.

"I came across a lot of interesting cases," I said. "But I'm confident this summer will be as normal as they come."

"Yes," Ursula said through gritted teeth. "I most certainly hope so."

I couldn't imagine how much stress it put on her every time I found a dead body or missing appendage. It would make me feel bad, except I hadn't asked to find them.

"I'm Ben—Ranger Three. I love Christmas music year-round, and my family is everything to me." Ben may have looked imposing with his massive stature and huge muscles, but he was a gentle giant. "It's been a pleasure to train summer rangers *almost* every year." He glanced my way.

I glared at him, then laughed.

"Nah, I'm just kidding," he said. "It's been fun every year."

"Hi." the woman next to Ben stood up, pushing her braid over her shoulder. "I'm Tatiana. I know I'm not as young as most of you, but I was a ranger in Florida for many years. After I retired, I moved here. But retirement is boring. So here I am."

"We're very excited to have your experience, Tatiana," Ursula said. "George, would you like to go next?"

The man next to Nikki stood as if his joints hurt with every movement.

What was Ursula up to? Why would she hire this guy?

"As Ursula said, my name is George." His voice was

harsher than I expected. "I'm a retired police officer from the Prairie City Police Department."

A retired park ranger *and* a retired cop? I was sensing a trend.

Nikki waited as if George might say more, but instead, he simply sat without making eye contact with anyone.

"I'm Nikki." She stood on her long legs and tucked a stray piece of her auburn hair behind her ear. "Like Rylie, I was a summer ranger last year and was hired on full-time last fall, but I was also a summer ranger five summers before as well. I manage most of the events and expect everyone to be on their best behavior during said events."

If it wasn't for how scary Nikki could be, I'm sure most of the rangers would have groaned or at least rolled their eyes. But Ursula looked pleased with Nikki's attitude. Probably because they were practically the same person.

Thankfully, Nikki and I had become friendlier over the past months. We definitely didn't start that way. Especially when she started dating my high school sweetheart, with whom I had recently tried to reconnect.

But that was neither here nor there because I'm engaged, Luke and Nikki broke up, and Luke went to the Middle East to teach people to be cops or something.

"I'm Sondra," the woman next to Antonio said. "I am not a retired cop or park ranger. I don't have a degree in environmental engineering. But I am happy to be here."

That was it.

She sat down without sharing a single piece of personal information.

The room was quiet for a moment before Ursula chimed in.

"Antonio, would you like to go next?"

Antonio leaned back in his chair as if he were on the cover of a romance novel. All he needed was to take off his shirt and grow out his hair. Or maybe put on a cowboy hat.

I shook my head to remove the mental picture.

Engaged.

I'm engaged.

And Antonio was the last man I should have been fantasizing about.

"I am Antonio," he said in his deep Italian voice, not bothering to stand. "I like long walks on the beach . . . in a uniform and a bulletproof vest. I have been here too many years to count, but I greatly enjoy this job."

Ursula didn't seem to enjoy his joke about the walks on the beach, but Victoria giggled next to me.

"Thank you." Ursula looked around. "That's everyone."

Greg motioned from her side, but she ignored him. He was too much of a gentleman to butt in, even if she had overlooked his introduction.

"You might meet Dusty and Seamus at some point. They're our trail rangers, but occasionally they come to the reservoirs to help," Ursula said. "Otherwise, you're good to go. I'm having lunch catered for everyone today. It will be in the banquet hall at noon. Dismissed."

I looked at my phone. It was only eight-thirty. At least I'd gotten an extra shot of espresso in my latte.

"Where to first?" Victoria stood with an excited grin on her face.

"You've seen the shop, I take it?" I stood up but still couldn't hold eye contact. It wasn't as if I was mad that she'd been the reason my ex cheated on me, I just didn't like the person she was. Maybe she didn't know Troy had a girlfriend when she met him, but she definitely could have figured it out the moment she walked into our bedroom. I mean, there were pictures of us on the nightstand.

"I've seen most of the reservoir. Actually, I've seen most of all the city parks. I did my internship with my aunt."

"You probably know them better than I do, then." I started down the spiral staircase toward where we parked the big black ranger trucks.

When we got inside the truck, she leaned over and whispered. "Can you take me to where you found the body in the trap?"

"You don't have to whisper," I said. "They can't hear you."

The other rangers were ushering their summies into their trucks.

"And no. I'm not supposed to be doing anything like that anymore. As far as I'm concerned, there were no crimes committed in the parks over the past year."

She sat back in her seat with a huff.

"Seatbelt," I reminded before pulling out of the shop. I almost let out a laugh as she strapped herself in. A mere seatbelt seemed insufficient for the rollercoaster ride of a summer I suspected we were about to have.

3

After spending nearly the entire morning driving around listening to Victoria's constant stream of babble, I finally got the nerve to ask, "Have we met somewhere? You look really familiar."

She shook her head. "I definitely would have remembered if I'd have met the famous Rylie Cooper."

"Famous?" I laughed.

"You had a viral video last year."

"Not my finest moment."

Being bitten by a snake wasn't fun.

Being bitten by a snake in the middle of a crowd with a hundred cell phone cameras pointed at me was even less fun.

"I thought it was great. You took charge when that other ranger was too scared. Can you show me how to do that with a snake?"

"You'll go through snake handling in your training," I said. "Hey, it looks like it's almost lunchtime. We better head toward the banquet hall."

"Already?" Her shoulders slouched, and she stopped talking for the first time in three hours.

"Don't worry. You have all summer to get out there."

"But I don't have all summer with you."

This girl was borderline obsessive.

"I'm not that great," I said. "Trust me."

"At least one person thinks you are," she said, pointing at my engagement ring. "That ring is huge. He must really love you."

"He does, but I'm sure the size of the ring doesn't indicate—"

"Of course, it does," she said. "My boyfriend better get me a ginormous ring."

I cringed inside. Was she talking about Troy? Why hadn't I considered the possibility that they'd still be together?

"Do you think you'll get engaged soon?" I asked as calmly as I could.

"I better be. I've waited long enough."

"How long is long enough?" My insides tightened, waiting for the answer.

"About a year and a half now," she said. "It's kind of long-distance, but he'll move wherever I get a *real* job."

She had to be talking about Troy. If she was, that meant he'd been cheating on me at least six months before I'd found out.

She was also in for a rude awakening. Troy and I had been together for five years, and he never so much as mentioned marriage. Looking back now, I should have known better.

"Ooh, who's that?" Victoria pointed to the seemingly deserted playground.

"Who's who?" I searched for what she might be talking about.

"That weird guy under the slide."

I squinted to find the same guy I'd had Ben chat with the day before. "Ugh. He's back."

"Should we talk to him?" Victoria was practically hopping out of her seat with excitement.

We hadn't had any contact with anyone yet. I didn't know if we were supposed to since she hadn't gone through any of the training, but I couldn't just leave some pothead under the slide. What if he hurt someone?

"I'll talk to him," I said. "You just observe, okay?"

She nodded so hard I thought her bun might come off the top of her head.

It didn't.

It stayed in its perfect erect position. Part of me wanted to ask what kind of hairspray she used, but my pride squashed that thought almost immediately. I ran a hand over my braided hair. It didn't seem like it was sticking out *too* much.

"Sir, is everything okay?" I asked.

The man was clutching his knees, rocking back and forth, muttering something to himself.

"Sir?" I asked.

He glanced over at me, and his eyes widened. "It-it's you."

He pointed a finger at me but then shifted it slightly to my right until he was pointing at Victoria.

"Do you know him?" I asked her.

She shook her head. "No."

"The wolf lady. You're the wolf lady." He tried to stand up but smacked his head on the underside of the slide. "You cursed me," he yelled, keeping his gaze on Victoria. "I can't walk. You cursed me."

"Sir, you're not cursed," I said. "You're underneath a slide."

Victoria looked petrified.

"If you come out, you'll see you can walk perfectly fine." I took a step toward him and kept my hand over the can of pepper spray on my belt.

Just in case.

He glared at me. "She cursed me, and you're not doing anything 'bout it."

"This woman—" I pointed at Victoria "—is a summer park ranger. She's not in uniform, but she is not a wolf lady. Right?" I turned to get Victoria to back me up.

But before she could confirm, the guy came charging at us. I pulled my pepper spray from my belt, but couldn't get to the trigger fast enough.

His shoulder hit my left arm with as much force as my youngest nephew might muster. Then he was on the ground.

"You cursed me too," he yelled from the fetal position on the ground. I looked around. Thankfully, no one else was around. I could only imagine what that would have looked like to my YouTube fans.

"She didn't curse you," Victoria said, finally finding her voice. "And neither did I. We're not wolf ladies."

Her voice was so sweet and calm. He looked up at her with tears in his eyes. "I'm sorry if I hurt your friend."

"You didn't hurt me," I said. "And we're just co-workers."

"Whoa, did you just body slam that guy?" A voice came from behind me.

I turned to find Tatiana gaping at me with Ben behind her.

"No," I said almost too quickly. "He charged me and then fell."

"Seriously, Ansel?" Ben stood next to the guy who was still lying on the ground. "Didn't we talk about this yesterday?"

"I know, I know," he said. "I just wanted to come back and see if she was here."

"The wolf lady?" Ben asked.

Ansel side-eyed Victoria but said nothing.

"Why don't you ladies head over to the banquet hall and get some food," Ben said. "I'll get Ansel situated."

"Shouldn't we stay and watch?" Tatiana asked. "For training purposes?"

Ben shrugged. "I don't see why not." He turned his attention to Ansel. "Let me help you up." He held out a hand and practically picked Ansel up to a stand. This guy was a twig—his dreadlocks looked like the heaviest things on his body. No wonder he couldn't properly charge into me. I was just glad I hadn't used my pepper spray on him.

"Did you walk in through the gate again?" Ben asked him.

"Yeah, dude. I can't drive like this." He laughed at himself, but still keeping an eye on Victoria.

"I want you to walk back through the gate and get a ride home," Ben said, his deep voice soothing. "And remember, getting high underneath a slide on a children's playground is not the best idea."

"I didn't get high here. I wouldn't do that." Ansel put a hand over his heart. "I care about the kids. I'm here to protect them."

"I know you care." Ben started walking with him toward the gate. Victoria and Tatiana followed while I stayed back.

"You'll get the wolf lady, right?" Ansel looked back at Victoria.

"We'll keep an eye out for her."

"Good, man, good," Ansel said with a nod. "I'll see you later."

Ben stopped, and Ansel kept ambling toward the gate.

"Should we watch and make sure he gets out okay?" Tatiana asked.

"He will, but he'll be back," Ben said.

"Why don't you call PD and have him locked up?" Tatiana asked. "Seems like releasing him could be a liability."

"I'll give dispatch a call here in a minute and let them know he's heading out of the park. If the police want to talk to him, they'll know where to find him."

Tatiana nodded.

"We should eat," Ben said. "I'm starving."

He and Tatiana walked several paces ahead of Victoria and me.

"That was super cool how you leveled that guy," Victoria whispered.

"I didn't level him," I said. "He was a bag of bones. He

practically knocked himself out. Did you know him or something? He seemed to be suspicious of you."

"Nope." She shrugged. "Never seen the guy before today."

She also said that about me, but I let it go.

We were silent until we approached the door Ben held patiently for us.

"You know back there when you said we were just co-workers?" Victoria said.

"Yeah."

"Do you think maybe someday we could become friends?"

I sucked in a breath. "Maybe."

4

"I've updated the schedule," Greg said when we were all seated with catered street tacos in front of us. "The summies—er—summer rangers will be in training the rest of the week. Tomorrow we will go over the basics in the morning and do the pepper spray course in the afternoon."

George sat forward and smiled. I held the summie pepper spray course record from last year, but it was entirely possible he'd break it being an ex-cop and all.

"For the full-timers," Greg continued. "We will have baton training—a refresher for most of you. Nikki and Rylie, you'll be taking the test at the end of the day to get certified."

Only full-time rangers had batons. None of us had guns because we weren't certified police officers, which was fine by me. I had no desire to carry a gun.

"Greg, I'm not sure I will be able to attend the training tomorrow," Nikki said. "I need to be available to facilitate set-up for the event on Saturday. Taking today off was a stretch, but I really need the rest of the week to get ready."

Greg glanced at Ursula.

"If you don't have this training, you can't carry a baton for another year," Ursula said.

"That's fine by me," Nikki said. "I haven't needed one yet. I can wait until next summer."

"Then it's settled," Ursula said. "And while we're on the subject of the event."

The rangers shifted in their seats. It was no secret the rangers disliked the events. They were a pain. They often overcrowded the reservoir, leaving our regular patrons unhappy. And vocal. But the events brought in more money than the regular patrons. More money *and* publicity.

"There will be a great deal of press covering this event. This is not just some small-time author book signing. It's a New York Times Bestselling Author book signing. People will be in costume. Prepare yourselves. You do not want to be caught on camera doing anything unprofessional."

She looked right at me when she said this.

I felt a blush rise up the back of my neck.

"With that being said, Greg, you may continue your discussion about the schedules," Ursula said.

"Thank you, Ursula. I'm sure everyone will be just as professional as they always are," he said with his grandfatherly smile. "Starting this weekend, the summer rangers will shadow their full-timer for two weeks. During the event Saturday, Ben will have George and Tatiana so Nikki can focus on her event duties. All the full-timers will have grading rubrics, and as long as all the boxes are checked after two weeks, the summer rangers will move onto working alone."

Two weeks?

My stomach dropped. I hadn't had to spend two weeks under supervision. And a grading rubric? Ugh. It was bad enough I'd have to work with Victoria all summer, but having to supervise her for two entire weeks?

That might kill me.

Lunch adjourned far too quickly, and Victoria and I were back in the ranger truck circling the park.

"Sorry, my aunt's so hard on you," Victoria said.

"You don't have to apologize. I'm sure it hasn't been easy dealing with all the messes I've made over the past year."

"You didn't make the messes." Victoria's voice was filled with frustration. "You didn't kill anyone. You just found the bodies. If it wasn't you, it would have been someone else."

"But I investigated. I stuck my nose into the cases when I should have let the police handle it."

"It sounds like the police—or one specific officer— wanted you there to help."

She was talking about Luke—how she knew about Luke was beyond me. And he *had* wanted my help. At least with the first case.

"Still, I'm not a police officer. If another case comes along, I'll absolutely be keeping my nose out of it."

Victoria crossed her arms over her chest and turned her gaze to the trail ahead of us. "If it wasn't for you, they never would have solved those cases, and you know it."

I didn't know where she was getting this information, but it wasn't entirely true. "Tell me more about yourself," I said, trying to change the subject. "You have a degree in environmental engineering. That sounds hard."

"It wasn't really. Just a lot of math and science."

Smart and humble.

Yuck.

"Why'd you choose that path?"

"I wanted to do something with nature, but I didn't want to just be in wildlife or recreation management. I wanted to actually use my brain."

Ouch.

My degree was in parks and recreation management.

"But you wanted to work as a park ranger?" Didn't sound like the job an environmental engineer would want.

"For now." She looked down at her nails, utterly unaware that she had insulted me. "Between you and me, my aunt got me the job. Said it would be easy money while I apply for jobs I really wanted."

I tightened my grip on the wheel. I couldn't let her get to me. But every part of me wanted to backhand her.

"What jobs do you *really* want?" I tried not to grit my teeth.

She glanced over at me. "Are you okay?"

I took a deep breath. "I'm fine."

"You don't look fine." She clapped a hand over her mouth. "Oh my goodness. Do *you* have a degree in recreation?"

I couldn't bring myself to nod.

"I'm sorry." She tried—and failed—to hide a laugh. "I just assumed you were one of the smarter ones. Not that having a degree in recreation makes you dumb," she quickly added. "Maybe you just really wanted to work in recreation."

We sat in silence for a few minutes. I didn't trust my mouth. If I said something mean to Ursula Vilago's niece, I might as well have handed in my resignation.

"I want to help save the planet," she whispered. "I want there to be resources for future generations."

I tried to push away my frustration. "Sounds like a noble cause."

5

"How was your first day with GG?" Shayla asked. I made dinner—spaghetti—and the two of us were cozied up on the couch waiting for our favorite show—*Love in Reality*—to begin.

"She's awful," I said. "She has a degree in environmental engineering and proceeded to tell me I was dumb because I have a degree in recreation."

"She called you dumb?"

"Not outright, but basically. She also told me she and Troy have been together for a year and a half. That means he'd been cheating on me for way longer than I thought."

"And she didn't recognize you?"

"Nope," I said. "I even asked her if we'd ever met, and she said she would have remembered meeting me because I went viral."

Shayla winced.

"Yeah. So I'm her dumb hero or something."

"Dumb hero?" Shayla chuckled.

"She acts like she idolizes me. She gets mad when

Ursula puts me in my place. But she obviously doesn't realize that I was in the wrong working those cases."

"In the wrong seems pretty harsh," Shayla said. "It's not like Luke told you to stay out of it."

"He did on the last one. And so did you."

"But if you'd stayed out of it, you wouldn't have gotten your sweet new ride."

"I do like Chery Anne the Second."

"How is Selena? Have you heard from her recently?"

Selena had been a missing person until her prosthetic arm surfaced at Shadow Trail Reservoir a few months ago. I found the arm, then her, but she had actually been in hiding rather than missing.

"She's doing well. It was a blow to find out Elodie's baby was Cedric's, but they're working it out."

"Elodie's baby was Cedric's?" Shayla gaped at me.

"Apparently, they had a one-night thing, and she ended up pregnant." I shrugged. "Turns out, Jacob was telling the truth when he told her he couldn't have kids."

Jacob was Selena's abusive ex-husband, who had taken up with Elodie after Selena disappeared. When Elodie found out Selena was still alive, she murdered Jacob so he wouldn't try to go back to his ex.

"It was a blessing in disguise," I said. "Since the baby wasn't Jacob's, Selena didn't have to fight Elodie for the estate. And to add insult to injury for Elodie, since Elodie will spend the rest of her life in prison, Selena is now raising Elodie's baby."

"It sounds like a soap opera," Shayla laughed. "How did Elodie think she would get away with it? Cedric's black and Jacob's not. Doesn't the baby look at all like his father?"

"I don't know that Elodie knew for sure." I shrugged and took a bite.

"Ooh, it's starting," Shayla said, turning the volume up on the TV. "This show has gotten so much better since they hired that new producer. I can't wait to see the engagement."

"Speaking of engagement," I said. "Have you and Seamus decided on a date for your Ireland trip?"

Shayla paled. "Next month."

"Are you ready?"

"To get married?" Shayla asked.

"To say yes."

"I love Seamus. I want to be with him forever. But . . ."

"But what?"

"How did you know Garrett was the right guy for you?"

I took a sip of my ice tea. "How could he not be? Have you seen him?"

She smiled. "He is pretty perfect."

"He's good with my nephews, he's gorgeous, and he has a fantastic job. Plus, he puts up with my crap."

"You need to lighten up on yourself," Shayla said. "You're not as bad as you make yourself out to be."

I shrugged. "It probably wasn't easy worrying his significant other might get herself killed."

"Seamus worries about that too."

"You're a good officer. He knows that." I smiled. "But keep pushing around that baby carriage, and he might get ideas."

"Speaking of the baby carriage, do you want to go shopping for a baby with me on Sunday?"

I chuckled. "Shopping for a baby."

Shayla paused the TV and waited with her eyebrows raised, waiting for me to stop laughing.

"Come on, that's funny," I said, trying to regain my composure. "Shopping for a baby." I lost it again. I laughed so hard my side cramped.

"I'll just have Bella go with me," Shayla said then took a bite of her spaghetti.

"I thought you had a baby."

"That one might have had a bit of an accident."

"What kind of accident?" I couldn't wait to hear this.

Shayla looked up at the ceiling as if she didn't want to tell me. "I accidentally ran it over."

"With your car?"

"It wasn't my finest moment, okay? I got distracted, and the next thing I know, I have a baby doll with a flattened plastic head."

"That should scare Seamus off the baby train."

Her face lit up. "You're right. It would."

"I do want to go baby shopping, though." I stopped laughing. "I've never been baby shopping before."

Shayla laughed. "It is kinda funny."

"Just promise I can babysit when you need to work," I joked.

"You can be the godmother," Shayla managed to say between her giggles.

"I'll do everything I can to make sure that baby has the best possible life if something should happen to you." I put on a serious face. "Just don't run over my godchild."

We were still laughing when Seamus walked through the door.

"What is going on? I can hear yeh all the way in the parking lot."

"We're just talking about picking out a baby for Shayla," I said, my laughter coming to a halt.

"Not a real baby," Shayla added quickly. "Just a baby for the carriage for rollerblading. I may have run over the last one."

"The both of yeh are crazy," Seamus said. "But if we're pickin' out a baby, don't yeh think I should be there? As the father?"

Shayla stopped laughing altogether. "Uh—well—"

"I'm just codding yeh."

"Codding?" I asked. "Like the fish?"

"Joking," Shayla translated. "He's joking." I could hear the thank God in her tone.

Seamus kissed Shayla on the top of the head.

"There's spaghetti on the stove," I said. "We're watching *Love in Reality*."

"Great," Seamus said in his least amused tone. "I think I'll take a shower quick."

When he was out of earshot, I whispered, "He'll be a good dad one day."

"Yeah." Shayla smiled. "He will be."

Her face glowed with happiness. If only I could be that excited about the thought of settling down and having kids.

6

"Using a baton is not like using a sword," Seamus said from the head of the classroom.

We all had our batons extended to go through the practice moves. We'd already gone over how the telescoping batons worked. To get them locked in their fully extended positions, you had to flick them down toward the ground. To make them collapse back into themselves so they'd fit in the holsters on our belts, you hit them against the ground.

"When yeh hit someone with a baton, yeh want to go for the extremities. The arms, hands, and legs." He demonstrated each hit to a foam mat Antonio held. "Pair up and practice these hits."

Greg wasn't there since he was doing the summie training. Ben and Dusty paired up, leaving Antonio as the only one for me to practice with.

Antonio seemed just as awkward as I was. Since we'd kissed on Christmas Eve, we pretty much avoided each other.

"Give me your best shot." Antonio held the mat against the side of his leg, bracing for impact.

I hit the mat with the baton.

"That was very wimpy." Antonio repositioned the bag. "Do not just use your arms. Pivot your hips."

I could feel the blush rise into my cheeks at the mention of my hips.

I hit the mat again, trying to turn my hips with the motion.

"Better," he said. "Now put your right foot forward instead of your left. It'll give you more reach and make it easier to pivot."

I switched legs and struck the mat again.

"You are a natural," Antonio said. "Now, let's try the arms."

He held the mat up, and I struck down on it as Seamus had demonstrated.

"Keep your left hand up for protection. This guy will do anything he can to get the best of you."

I brought the baton down again, keeping my left hand up.

"Yeh might wonder why I'm not teaching yeh to strike the wanker's head," Seamus said as he walked around the room. "First, if he ducks, yeh'll have thrown a strike that'll leave yeh off balance, and he'll get the upper hand. Second, if he doesn't, yeh'll likely be answering to the courts about why yeh needed to use deadly force."

I swiped down at the mat Antonio held, and he smiled at me from above the bag. "I bet you have been waiting for your chance to hit me."

"Why would I want to hit you?"

"Because I almost messed up your relationship with the accountant." He repositioned the mat to the side of his leg.

I looked around to make sure no one heard. The only person in the room who knew Antonio and I had kissed besides the two of us was Seamus, and I wanted to keep it that way. I adjusted my stance and swung. "I was just as much to blame as you." I hit the mat again. "Actually, more so," I whispered. "I was in a relationship. I shouldn't have put either of us in the position."

"Hit harder."

I did.

"Up top." He put it up high.

I hit.

"Good Rylie, yeh're a natural," Seamus said as he walked by.

"She hits hard too," Antonio said with a laugh.

"Take a break," Seamus said, and we dropped our batons to our sides.

"Now, I also need to teach yeh when to stop," Seamus said. "At some point, yeh have to stop beatin' a person. If they've gone to the ground, stop. If they've backed off, stop. Tell them to stay back and call for help if yeh haven't pushed your emergency button already. If they come at yeh again, resume hittin' or change to pepper spray."

He was primarily talking to me since I was the one who hadn't already gone through the training.

"Any questions?" he asked.

I shook my head, no.

"Good, then let's take the test and get out of here."

The test was a breeze. I *was* a natural, after all. Not

that I'd ever use the skill, but it was nice to know I could protect myself if need be.

"Come outside, quick," Carmen—the park office manager—barged into the room as Seamus was grading my written test.

We raced outside.

It took me a minute to figure out what Carmen was so excited about. Until Victoria came trotting up the beach, her face only slightly redder than usual.

Greg patted her on the back. "Congratulations, kiddo! You beat Rylie's record!"

Every bit of pride I had from doing so well with baton training rushed out of me.

Ben patted me on the back. "It was bound to happen sometime."

But why did it have to be her? What happened to George?

I glanced around. George sat at a picnic table with tears streaming down his red face. He'd already done the course.

I pushed my face into a grin when I saw Ursula observing.

Or rather, completely fangirling—waving her arms in the air cheering for Victoria.

"How'd I do?" Victoria asked Greg, Ranger One. She didn't even look tired.

"You did fantastically." He leaned in but didn't lower his voice. "Are you secretly immune to pepper spray?"

Victoria giggled, tipping her head back as if he'd just made the funniest joke ever. The other summies—Tatiana and Sondra—looked like they'd just watched Old Yeller on repeat. Their eyes were as red as ripe tomatoes and swollen almost completely closed.

Victoria hadn't even ruined her mascara.

Maybe Greg hadn't sprayed her good enough? Somehow, she cheated. I knew it. There was no way she could beat me.

Though, she *had* gotten my boyfriend of five years to cheat on me.

Ugh.

I hated that I hated her so much.

7

Werewolves, vampires, and other strange beings had overtaken the park. This *New York Times* Bestselling Author had her own security detail, arrived in a limo, and looked like she had just stepped out of *Vogue* magazine.

In a sea of monsters, she was a precious gem polished to the nth degree.

"Have you read her books?" Victoria asked me from the passenger side of the truck as we overlooked the chaotic scene.

"No, have you?"

Victoria shook her head no, her bun once again staying firmly on top of her head. "I hear they're good, but I'm not much of a reader. No time."

"I've read them. They're good." Logan Labrec came to stand at my window. A tiny thing with long dark hair, she was the girlfriend of Denver Broncos Quarterback, Eli Hudson.

"Hey, Logan," I said. "How's it going?"

"Pretty good." A large camera hung around her neck, and she held a tripod in her hand.

"Business or pleasure?" I pointed at the camera.

"Both," Logan said.

"I thought you covered sports."

Logan pulled the camera up to her eye and shot a couple of photos of the crowd. "I got benched."

"That sounds . . . ominous."

She put the camera down and raised one eyebrow at me. "Don't ask."

Victoria cleared her throat next to me.

"Oh yeah, this is Victoria Vilago, the summie I'm training."

"Nice to meet you." Victoria reached across me to shove her hand through the window.

Logan shook her hand once. "Pleasure."

"Ranger Six, Ranger Seven?" Nikki's voice came through the mic on my shoulder.

I clicked the button. "Go ahead."

"I need you and Fourteen down here to help with crowd control." I could see Nikki waving up at us.

Victoria was assigned badge number fourteen—*my* summie number—which didn't sit well with me. I knew it wasn't intentional, but still.

"We'll be right there," I said into the mic.

"Six clear," Nikki said, clearing the channel so other rangers could use it.

"I'll see you later," Logan said. "I have pictures to take. And maybe I'll get an autograph."

"Good luck." I jumped out of the truck and locked it. My belt was heavier with the baton on my left side. It pointed slightly in front of me so I could reach across and grab it with my right hand, extend it with a flick of the wrist, and use it if needed. I may have practiced a couple hundred times in front of my bedroom mirror.

"Is it heavy?" Victoria pointed at my baton.

"Not too bad."

"Can I hold it?"

There were way too many people around for her to be playing with a weapon she wasn't trained to use. "Maybe when we get back to the truck."

This seemed to satisfy her.

"Do you mind if I take a bathroom break and then meet you over there?" Victoria said, following me toward the crowd.

"That's fine. Just be quick," I said, and Victoria jogged off toward the bathrooms.

Nikki was the calm in the storm. Where vampires and werewolves pranced around with excitement, Nikki kept her hands lightly resting on her duty belt, her eyes peeled for trouble.

"Everything seems to be going well," I said. "Good job."

"It's not a good job yet. The event isn't even halfway over." Nikki's long red hair was twisted in a low chignon, her makeup perfect, and her nails a glossy pale pink. "I need you to make sure the barricades are still up past the playground. If it seems quiet, come back and check in with me."

"Will do," I said. The playground was right next to the bathrooms, so it would be easy to find Victoria even in a sea of people.

I moved past a group of expertly costumed werewolf ladies and walked over the hill toward the playground. It was empty.

The barricades were probably up, but I knew Nikki would ask if I actually *saw* them up, so I continued on to make sure.

A scream came from the other side of the playground. "Help!"

I took off running.

When I came around to where Victoria stood yelling, a familiar sight met my eyes.

"Not again," I muttered under my breath.

A woman's body lay at the feet of my nemesis.

As I hurried to meet Victoria, I pulled on a pair of rubber gloves. "Here," I handed Victoria a set when I reached her. "Put them on. Did you touch anything?"

She shook her head, no.

"What happened?" I asked.

"I-I don't know." Victoria looked up at me with a terrified expression on her face. "I came out of the bathroom, and she was just lying there."

I dropped to my knees, lowered my ear to her mouth, and looked down the length of her body for signs of breathing.

The woman—tall with blood matting her short blonde hair—had red marks all over her body. She wore short shorts, aviator sunglasses, and a tank as if she had been running the trail.

I couldn't detect any breath.

"Ranger Seven, Ranger Six," I said into my mic as I checked for a pulse.

"Six," Nikki said.

"Can you send the ambulance to the playground? We have an unconscious woman in need of immediate assistance."

It was a definite plus that every event required ambulance staff on-site.

"They're on their way," Nikki said. "Do we need PD?"

"Affirm," I said.

"Copy."

"Seven clear."

A crowd was gathering around us, their camera phones aimed directly at my face. Ursula was going to fire me.

"She did it," Ansel emerged from beneath the slide, pointing at Victoria. "Wolf lady did it."

"I'm not wolf lady," Victoria said, tears making her voice husky. "Stop calling me wolf lady."

"You killed her. Wolf lady killed her." He sounded more stoned today than he had been earlier in the week.

Victoria was in full-on sobbing mode now.

Ansel rushed back under the slide and pulled his knees up to his chest, rocking back and forth like a child.

"Do you want me to talk to him?" George asked from behind me, making me jump.

"No," I said. "I want you to meet the ambulance and direct them down here." I pointed to where the ambulance would be.

He nodded but looked like he didn't trust me enough to leave me at the scene alone.

A faint pulse tapped at my index finger.

The woman was alive.

I rechecked for breath. I couldn't be sure, but I thought I heard a tiny wheeze.

"Ansel, it's okay," I said in his direction. "Did you see the attack?"

"Wolf lady got her. I was asleep. She screamed. Wolf lady wouldn't stop. Awful." He was crying now.

"Was it one of the people in costume?" I asked.

The crowd gasped. Ninety percent of them were in costume.

But Ansel didn't answer.

He and Victoria continued crying.

The ambulance arrived on scene within minutes.

"Update?" One of the paramedics asked.

"She has a faint pulse and a bit of wheezing," I said. "Her ribs look like they might be broken, keeping her from getting a good breath." I got to my feet. "I'll deal with crowd control."

The paramedic nodded and took over.

Victoria stood staring at the woman, her face ghostly.

"If you need to throw up, go to the bathroom," I said.

"I don't." She peeled her puffy red eyes from the woman.

"What do you need?" George asked his eyes on a frozen Victoria.

"Help me with crowd-control," I said. "We need to keep people back."

I held my arms out as wide as they would go and shouted orders at the people around. "Everyone back. We need to give the paramedics space to work."

Slowly the hoard of devoted fans—cell phones and all

—moved back. I looked to my left, and George was doing the same as me.

Logan pushed her way through the crowd, her camera taking in the scene with rapid clicks of her finger.

"How close can I get?" she asked.

"No closer than you already are," I said. "Do you really need to take photos? It's pretty gruesome."

"Sex and gore. That's all the fans want anymore." She shrugged. "And I'll be doing a live broadcast."

That was my cue. I had no desire to be part of a live broadcast. "Just stay behind the barricades," I said.

Ben and Tatiana were moving the wooden barricades to provide a solid barrier between the scene and the crowd.

The police still weren't there when the ambulance flipped on its lights and screamed out of the park

"Do you think she'll make it?" Victoria asked, finally tear-free.

I shrugged. "I hope so." I turned to Ben. "Think you could go chat with Ansel? He seems to like you. He's taking this pretty badly." I lowered my voice so Victoria couldn't hear. "He thinks Victoria did this."

"Did she?" Ben asked.

"I don't think so," I said. However, she had been gone when it happened.

"Okay, sure," Ben said. "He probably has to stick around so the police can interview him, right?"

"I don't know how reliable he is." I held up two fingers and made a motion as if I were smoking a joint. "But I wouldn't let him go until PD says it's okay."

"Ah, okay," Ben said. "Keep an eye out for my summies."

"All right, everyone. There's nothing more to see," I addressed the crowd. "Please make your way back to the event area to get your books signed and meet the author."

"Don't tell them, but the park's locked down," a deep bullfrog voice came from behind me. "No one in or out."

I turned to see Jerry, a Prairie City Police Officer. He and I had gotten familiar since he had been Luke's partner before Luke shipped off to the Middle East.

"I hear there's a witness?"

"Ben's talking to him." I pointed toward the slide where Ansel still huddled beneath.

"Anything else I should know?" he asked.

"Not my thing to investigate crimes," I said.

He raised an eyebrow.

"I'm a changed woman."

I thought he almost smiled—his handle-bar mustache twitching slightly—before he walked away.

"Come on," I said to Victoria, who still looked like she might faint. "Let's go see if Nikki needs anything."

8

The police did a masterful job of talking to everyone without causing any panic. By the time the event concluded, they had spoken to nearly everyone, but from what I gathered—not that I was purposely trying to collect information—they'd found nothing.

They'd spoken with Victoria for over an hour, but she swore up and down she knew nothing. She'd begged me to stay with her while they asked questions.

Whoever beat that woman was either a master at hiding, a brilliant liar, or was long gone.

"Did you get everything you need?" I asked Logan as she was packing up her camera.

"More than I needed. I always take way too many photos and videos, but it gives me more to work with after the fact."

"So you do live broadcasts *and* post-event videos?"

"The assignments I've gotten lately don't exactly

warrant live coverage. I mean, who wants to watch an author sign thousands of books live?"

She had a point.

"We should catch up soon," I said when I saw Ursula making her way toward me. "I want to hear about what happened."

She nodded.

When Victoria saw Ursula, she practically launched herself into her aunt's arms.

"Oh sweetie, are you okay?" Ursula had never seemed warm and nurturing until now. "I heard they questioned you. As if they thought you might hurt someone."

"It was awful. But Rylie stayed with me the entire time." Victoria sobbed. "That poor woman, she didn't deserve that."

"Of course, she didn't." Ursula looked up at me. Her voice cooled when she said, "You're staying away from this case, right?"

"Yes," I said. "I'm leaving it to the professionals."

"Good," she said and went back to comforting Victoria.

"Rylie was amazing," Victoria said. Her next words were too quiet for me to make out, but I think she said something about being too hard on me.

Ursula didn't respond. I didn't need her to. I knew what they expected of me. I didn't want to be a cop. I didn't want to carry a gun. And because of that, I couldn't investigate crimes. Plain and simple.

"Any word on the victim's state?" Ben asked, coming up next to me.

"That's why I'm here. I've been at the hospital

awaiting news," Ursula said. "She died in surgery. There was nothing they could do. The damages were too great."

With that, Victoria's knees buckled, and she almost took Ursula down with her. I hurried to help her up. "Maybe you should go home. I can finish the shift by myself." If she had hurt that woman, she was a brilliant actress.

"No," Victoria said in a weak but firm voice. "I'll be okay. I'm sorry. I shouldn't act like this."

"Most people don't react well to death—especially violent death," Ben said. "Rylie's just the special kind that can handle it." He smiled at me. "The first time she and I found a body—the one in the catfish trap—I was a total disaster."

"It's true," I said, trying to lighten the mood. "He was."

He nudged me with his elbow. "You weren't supposed to agree with me."

"Even tough guys can have weaknesses," I said.

Ben puffed out his muscular chest before letting the air out of his lungs with a slight laugh. "I guess you're right."

"Are you sure you want to complete your shift?" Ursula asked Victoria. "No one would blame you if you wanted to come home."

"If I'm going to do this, I need to be tougher." Victoria's voice was stronger. "It'll be okay."

"Everything's done here." A voice behind me instantly made my insides curdle.

I turned to see Detective Harry Bryant.

"Hello, Rylie," he said. "It's good to see you."

"Pleasure's all mine," I said, trying not to sound too sarcastic.

He smirked then turned his attention back to Ursula. "We've taken the man from the playground into custody."

"As in, arrested him?" Ben asked. "Ansel's a good guy. You can't possibly think he did it."

"He had a baseball bat with him," Bryant said. "Under the slide."

I'd never seen Ansel with a baseball bat, but a bat definitely could have caused the damage I'd seen.

"We'll test it for blood," Bryant said. "In the meantime, if he's released and ends up back here, please call us immediately."

Ben nodded but looked frustrated that they'd arrested Ansel.

"As far as the woman," Bryant continued. "She had no identification on her, not even a cell phone. I know she was pretty badly beaten up, but did anyone recognize her?"

He looked around at the group of rangers.

One by one, everyone shook their heads. The only person not making eye contact was Victoria, who still looked like she might faint or vomit or both.

"If you think of anything else, please give me a call." He handed each of the rangers a card.

"It's programmed in my phone," I said when he held a card out for me.

"That's right. It is," he said. "It was generous of Selena to give you a new phone."

"And a car," I said.

"You deserved the car," he said. "Especially after what she did to your old one."

Just the thought of the damages to Cherry Anne—my old Mustang—made me cringe. But having a brand new, top of the line replacement helped. Plus, I'd been able to donate the original Cherry Anne to a charity.

"Cherry Anne lives on in spirit through Cherry Anne the Second." I laughed. "Though she prefers to simply go by Cherry Anne."

Bryant looked at me like I'd grown another head. "Nice baton. When'd you get that?"

"Yesterday. I passed the test with flying colors."

"Just don't touch it," Victoria said, finally finding her voice. "She's a bit protective."

"You wouldn't let Victoria touch your baton?" Ursula said. "Why wouldn't you let Victoria touch your baton?"

I could hear the guys snicker beside me. I kept my face neutral even though I wanted to laugh right along with them.

"We were busy, but of course, she can—er—touch my baton."

The snickers grew slightly louder.

I pulled the baton out, flicked it into its locked position, and handed it to Victoria. She smiled at me the same way my older sister did when we were kids, and she got me in trouble with our parents.

She twirled it around gracefully, looking it up and down.

"If that's all, we should get ready to close up," I said, noting the sun dipping below the horizon.

No one objected.

"Ready?" I asked Victoria, who was still examining my baton.

"Yep," she said.

We walked to the truck in silence.

"Ouch," she said from the other side of the truck as I was getting in.

"Your baton bit me." Victoria laughed. "I smacked it on the ground to get it to close, but it didn't collapse properly."

She probably hadn't hit it hard enough.

"And when I tried to pull the small piece out of the top, it pinched me." She put her finger in her mouth. "Here, you do it."

I took the baton, stepped back out of the truck, hit it on the ground, collapsing it completely, and returned it to my belt.

She pulled her finger out of her mouth to examine it, blood bubbling up.

"Do you need a Band-Aid?" I asked.

"I'll be okay." She shoved her finger back in her mouth. "Do you really think Ansel beat her with his bat?"

I shook my head. "No. There's no way he had the strength or coordination. Remember when he charged me? I barely felt a thing."

"Maybe he was just faking it," she said, her words mumbled because her finger was still in her mouth.

"Maybe," I said. "He just doesn't seem like the type."

"She didn't deserve that," Victoria said for the second time.

"Did you know her?" I asked.

Victoria's head whipped around. "No. Of course, I didn't."

I raised my eyebrows. "Are you sure?"

She turned her focus to the hood of the truck. "Positive. Never seen her in my life. Now how do we close the reservoir?"

She was lying.

And if she was lying, did that mean she might have had something to do with the attack?

"You know—" I started the truck "—if you did know who she was, it would be good to tell the police so they can call her family. I know I'd want to know if one of my loved ones had died."

She didn't respond.

I pushed away my curiosity. I would not get in the middle of this investigation.

Even if my summie-slash-nemesis might be a murderer.

9

"And you think she knows—knew—knows—" Bella waved a hand in the air "—you know what I mean. But you think Victoria knows the identity of the woman?"

I had just told Bella and Shayla the story from the day before. Bella was married to Brock, a previous summie and current Prairie City cop. They recently had a little boy —Boyd—who Bella pushed in a stroller while she rollerbladed. Shayla was also pushing a stroller—albeit an empty one since we hadn't gone shopping for baby number two yet—and rollerblading.

"She seemed to. And it brings into question whether she may have had something to do with the attack." I was rollerblading with them—perfectly fine without a stroller to keep my balance, thank you very much. And even if I hadn't been, there was no way I'd be caught dead pushing an empty baby carriage. Or worse, one with a fake baby.

It was tricky with all the people on the trail, though. Especially all the people with their dogs.

Usually, people took their dogs to the dog park, but today there were tons of them on the trail around Alder Ridge Reservoir.

"That's a big accusation," Shayla said.

"It just didn't feel right," I said. "I don't know. Maybe they got in an argument, and things escalated. Ansel—the stoner under the slide—thought she did it. He's been calling her wolf lady since before all this."

"But he was stoned, right?" Bella asked.

"Yeah," I said. "I know, that makes him completely unreliable. I don't know. When Bryant—"

"*Detective* Bryant," Shayla corrected.

"When *Detective* Bryant interviewed her, she seemed sincere. So either she did nothing wrong, or she's an excellent liar. Either way, I'm staying out of it."

"And she still doesn't recognize you?" Bella asked. The rollerblading had paid off. She hardly looked like she had a baby only a couple of months ago.

"Apparently not," I said.

"I bet she's lying," Shayla said. "I mean, maybe not about the attack, but who forgets the face of a woman who catches you in bed with her cheating boyfriend?"

"True," I said. "But what does she have to gain by lying about not recognizing me?"

"If she came right out and admitted she was the one who ruined your relationship, she wouldn't exactly have a happy work environment," Bella said.

"And hypothetically, if she does remember you, did she go for a job as a summer ranger on purpose?" Shayla almost lost her balance but gripped the stroller more tightly and regained it.

I hadn't considered the fact that she might have gotten a job to get close to me.

"Keep your enemies closer?" Bella shrugged. "I mean, if Troy cheated on you with her, maybe she's paranoid he'd cheat on her with you."

"But I'm engaged." I held up my left hand, showing off my ring. "I have no interest in Troy."

"We know that," Shayla said. "But does Victoria?"

"She knows I'm engaged. She actually started talking about how her boyfriend better propose soon. If I know Troy, she's in for a long wait." I laughed.

Bella and Shayla exchanged looks.

"What?" I asked.

"What if he proposes?" Bella snuck a peek at her sleepy little guy. "Will you be okay?"

"Definitely," I said, though I could feel my blood pressure spike. "Like I said, I have no interest in Troy."

"Good," Shayla said. "Ooh, watch out."

A woman was coming at us with her four—yes four—huge dogs. All on leashes and perfectly well-mannered. That didn't mean they didn't take up the entire trail, though.

Shayla and I fell in behind Bella to make a line and take up the least amount of space possible.

The woman yelled out a command, and the dogs did the same.

My jaw dropped. Fizzy would never have behaved so well. Not for all the treats in the world. He was a free spirit. Hence, why I didn't take him on walks around the reservoir.

The woman—tall with a long braid wrapped around

the top of her head—waved as she passed, and we did the same.

I couldn't help but glance behind me to see if the dogs went back into spread formation after they passed us. But as I was looking, my wheel must have caught a rock, because the next thing I knew, I was tumbling to the ground.

The sting of road rash crept up my arm and the side of my face.

"Oh my goodness," Bella said, turning and coming back to me. Shayla wasn't quite so graceful, and it took her a bit longer. "Are you okay?"

I pushed myself up to a sit and examined my arm. Blood seeped out at a slow trickle. I gingerly touched my face. Only a small amount of blood transferred to my hand.

"I think so," I responded.

"Oh my God, that was the most epic fall ever." The one and only Victoria jogged up next to me. "It's too bad I didn't get it on video. You would have easily gone viral again."

I would do just about anything *not* to go viral again.

"Shayla, Bella," I said. "This is Victoria, the summie I'm training."

Both of my friends plastered smiles on their faces and shook Victoria's hand.

"It's so nice to meet Rylie's friends," Victoria said, her voice so high-pitched I wondered if the dogs might turn around and come back at us.

Victoria stuck out a hand. "Can I help you up?"

My pride made me want to stick my tongue out at her. But I also didn't want to be rude.

I took her hand, and she pulled with more strength than I expected.

But she pulled too hard. When my body came up, the wheels of my rollerblades spun back, and I ended up back on the ground—on my hands and knees this time.

"Damnit," I yelled out in pain. Now my knees were busted up too.

"I'm so sorry," Victoria said, still holding onto my hand. "Sometimes, I don't know my own strength." When I looked up into her eyes, it almost seemed like a challenge. But her expression flickered back to normal so quickly I could have been making it up in my head.

"It's okay." I pulled my hand away. "I can get up on my own. Thanks, though."

It took a couple of tries to get my balance, but finally, I managed to return to the upright position. With rollerblades on, I was eye-to-eye with Victoria.

She bent down and picked up my straw fedora. "Here." She held it out to me. "Cute hat."

"Thanks." I plopped it back on top of my frizzy hair. I hadn't done anything with it when I'd gotten out of the shower, and it was surely sticking up every which way. Victoria smirked, her own hair perfectly smooth in two long French braids. What was it with everyone having such perfectly plaited hair?

"All right, I'll just keep on my run," Victoria said. "It was nice meeting you both."

Shayla and Bella returned the sentiment and then turned their attention on me.

"Are you okay? Should we head back?" Shayla asked. "You're not bleeding too bad, but I'm sure that hurts like the dickens."

It stung, but not any more than my pride. "I'm fine. It's not far back to the parking lot."

We started down the trail, more slowly than before.

"Maybe you need a stroller too," Shayla finally said, and she and Bella laughed.

I couldn't help myself. I laughed too. "I might need one, but there's no way I'll use one. No offense, Shay."

Shayla shrugged. "I'm not the one with road rash on ten percent of my body."

"Ugh, and of course, that's the moment perfect miss giraffe girl had to make her appearance. I just wish she was uglier or something. How can someone look so perfect during a run?" I sighed. "Did you know she beat my pepper spray course record? And her eyes didn't even look that red afterward."

"I'm sorry," Shayla said. "But she's not perfect. You're just as pretty as she is."

Bella nodded. "It's obvious Troy had a type. Tall, blonde, gorgeous."

I laughed. "Sure, whatever."

"It's true," Shayla said, her face brightening as if a lightbulb had fired up inside her skull. "That's so weird. I wonder if Seamus has a type."

"Do you think you'll meet his ex-wife when you go to Ireland?" Bella asked.

"I hope not," Shayla said. "That would be awkward."

We talked about Shayla's upcoming trip to Ireland the rest of the way back to our cars.

"Make sure you get that all cleaned up when you get home." Shayla pointed at my face. "And use lots of antibiotic ointment. If you don't have any, there's some in my bathroom."

"I have some," I said. "Thanks. I'm sorry I can't go baby shopping with you."

We had made plans to buy her baby after the trial rollerblading with a stroller trip.

"It's okay," Shayla said. "Just promise you'll babysit every once in a while."

"Deal," I said, not sure if she was serious.

"See you later, Bella," I called out as Bella transferred the car seat from the stroller to the car.

She waved goodbye and closed the car door gently. "Don't let giraffe girl get in your head. She has your leftovers. In the long run, she did you a favor. She kept you from getting stuck with a cheating piece of poo-poo."

"Thanks."

Bella always had a way of seeing the bright side. It was probably why she and Shayla were such good friends.

And she was right, Victoria was just the sloppy seconds and if she knew that, that might make her dangerous. Maybe that's why she jerked me up so hard. She had no intention of actually helping me to my feet.

For the next couple of weeks, if not the entire summer, I'd have to watch my back.

Nikki stood at the front of the room, going over how the event went. Mondays weren't typically busy, and all the rangers were required to attend the debriefings.

I gingerly touched the patches of road rash on my face. They were pretty minor compared to my arm, but they made my head pound.

"Any questions?" Nikki said after giving the final numbers.

I looked around. She hadn't said a word about the woman who had been beaten to death.

It would have been better if someone else asked the question, but the guys all had dazed looks on their faces. They likely hadn't even heard her ask if they had questions.

I raised my hand.

"Rylie," Nikki said as if she was my third-grade teacher.

"Were they able to determine the identity of the woman we found?"

Nikki raised an eyebrow. "You're not asking for investigational purposes, are you?"

I knew that would be her first thought.

"Nope, just wanted to know."

"Someone from the event identified her," Nikki said. "Her name was Michelle something."

"What about Ansel?" Ben asked. "Did they release him?"

"I'm not sure. Ursula only told me about Michelle."

"He didn't do it," Ben said. "He was completely incapable."

I nodded. "When he charged me, it felt like a stiff breeze. Plus, he just didn't seem angry enough to hurt someone."

"But we'll leave that up to the police, *right*?" Nikki said.

"Yes," I said. "I can't afford to lose this job. I kinda like it here."

Ben smiled. "Even training a summie?"

I groaned. "She's horrible."

"She seems fine to me," Antonio spoke up.

"Just because she's gorgeous, doesn't mean she's not horrible." I glared at him.

"Why do you hate her so much?" Nikki asked. "Is it just because she's Ursula's niece?"

I glanced around. It was only Ben, Antonio, Nikki, and me. Greg was usually at the debriefings but was currently in the classroom teaching the summies.

"You have to keep this to yourselves, okay?"

They all nodded in agreement.

"Victoria is the reason I left the mountains. She's the woman I caught in bed with my ex-boyfriend."

Nikki gasped and clapped a hand over her mouth.

"Does she remember you?" Ben asked.

"I don't know. She claims we've never met, but sometimes I get a feeling she does." I looked down at my hands. "And from what I've gathered, she and Troy had been messing around longer than I thought. They're still together."

Antonio let out a low whistle. "That sucks."

"You're telling me," I said. "And I'm stuck with her for two more weeks. I wish I could get rid of her somehow."

"Get rid of who?" Victoria asked as she walked into the room, the rest of the summies and Greg behind her.

Antonio's eyes widened.

"No one," I said. "Just a neighbor. She's awful. She plays disco music all night. Loudly. I can't sleep because of it." I snapped my mouth shut. Verbal vomit as Troy would have said.

Troy.

The man who had betrayed me.

With her.

Yuck.

"She sounds awful," Victoria said, her expression looked as if she didn't quite believe me. "Anyway, I have news." Her tone went into high-pitched dog-whistle mode.

She held up her left hand. "Look how much he loves me."

Damn. My heart plummeted to my feet.

The ring was massive.

It was three times the size of mine.

"Congratulations." Ben glanced over at me.

"Thank you." She threw her arms around his neck, taking him aback. We weren't much of a hugging group, but within minutes she'd hugged every one of us. Me last.

"Now we're both engaged." She squeezed me so hard, I thought my ribs might break. "Isn't that exciting?"

Antonio, Nikki, and Ben watched as if they were ready to step between us when I snapped.

But strangely enough—now that my heart had climbed back into my chest from the initial shock—I didn't feel the way I thought I might. As much as I despised Victoria, Bella helped me realize I wouldn't be where I was without finding her and Troy together. I wouldn't even know Nikki or Antonio or Ben or Shayla or Bella. I would never have reconnected with Luke. And I wouldn't be engaged to the most wonderful man in the world. I'd still be in a dead-end relationship with a cheater.

Part of me wanted to warn Victoria. But she knew. She was there.

"I'm so happy for you," I said as she released me.

Antonio, Nikki, and Ben let out a collective sigh of relief as if they thought I might go all nutso and whack her or something.

"We can discuss wedding plans when we close tonight."

"Great," I said. "Can't wait." I hadn't even discussed wedding plans with Garrett yet.

"The summies are ready to go," Greg said. "They have their duty belts, radios, and badges."

Sure enough, Victoria was outfitted in a full uniform.

And she wore it well. Better than I had when I'd gotten my summie uniform. If it hadn't been for my mom's superb tailor skills, I would have been yanking my pants up all summer.

"We should probably get back out there," I said. "Ready?"

Victoria nodded.

"You okay?" Nikki whispered as I walked by.

"Never better," I replied.

There were only a few visitors in the park all evening. Victoria and I had taken up surveillance at the top of the dam, where a handful of fishermen tried their luck at landing a walleye.

"I still can't believe what happened to Michelle," I said as casually as I could.

"Yeah," Victoria said, her voice catching in her throat. "I can't believe she died."

"So you did know her?"

Victoria narrowed her eyes at me. "You tricked me."

"I just asked a question," I said. "How did you know her?"

"We dated the same guy a while back." She crossed her arms over her chest.

"At the same time?" Was being a home wrecker a habit of hers?

"No," she said. "Not at the same time. She dated him before I did."

"And you two became friends?" This story made no sense.

"Keep your enemies closer, right?" She looked me straight in the eye when she said it. A chill ran down my spine. If she'd dated a guy Michelle had and she'd killed Michelle, was I next?

I broke eye contact and glanced out over the lake. "How did your boyfriend feel about the two of you becoming friends?"

"He didn't care," she said. "As far as he was concerned, I was an upgrade."

Sounded like she was attracted to douchebags.

"An upgrade, huh?" Is that what she thought she was to Troy? Like she was so much better than me? "I think we should head back down to the offices and close up."

"Yep." She sat back in the seat and crossed her arms over her chest.

We didn't talk until we got down to the office area.

"Why don't you lock up the bathrooms by the playground," I said. "I'll arm the alarms in the offices."

Victoria shrugged and headed off toward the bathrooms.

I could feel my shoulders droop as I could finally let my guard down. I hadn't been this stressed in a long time. The offices were dark and empty. Part of me just wanted to sit in Carmen's chair and decompress in the silence.

I'd have to put the top down on the way home.

"Ranger—uh—I'm Fourteen to Ranger—uh—Rylie?" Victoria's voice came through the mic on my shoulder.

"Ranger Seven, go ahead, Fourteen."

"Yeah, Seven. Sorry." She unclicked her mic, and the radio went silent.

I waited a minute for her to continue before clicking the mic. "What did you need, Fourteen?"

She didn't answer.

The last time a ranger didn't answer right away, they'd found a dead body. Well, Shayla had found a decapitated body.

"Fourteen?" I said again as I turned and began to jog toward the bathrooms and playground. "Are you there?"

The radio was eerily silent.

"Do you need help over there, Seven?" Antonio's voice came through the mic. He was at Shadow Trail Reservoir, probably locking up as well.

"I don't know," I said into the mic. "Standby."

"Copy," Antonio said.

"Ranger Seven, Ranger Fourteen, do you copy?" I was flat running now. I'm sure the panic came through in my voice, but I didn't care.

"Oh sorry," Victoria finally said. "I must have turned the radio off when I was talking."

I slowed to a walk, the bathrooms in view. How could she have possibly turned off her radio?

"Are you in the bathrooms?" I asked.

"I'm at the playground. That's why I was calling," Victoria's voice was annoyed as if I was an idiot for not knowing that. "Ansel is back, and he's freaking out."

"Copy," I said. "I'll get PD on the phone. Are you code four?"

"What's code four?" Victoria asked.

"Okay. Are you okay?" It was my turn to be exasperated. Hadn't she gone through all of this in training?

"Other than him cowering under the slide screaming at me," she said.

I turned the corner and saw Victoria standing about ten feet away from where Ansel looked petrified.

"I didn't kill her," Victoria shouted.

"You-you're—" Ansel stammered.

"I'm not the wolf lady." Victoria seemed frustrated. "I didn't hurt Michelle. Sure we had our differences, but I won. I got the guy. If anything, she would have tried to hurt me."

"No way, man," Ansel replied. "I saw you."

I held back to listen to their exchange.

"You're stoned now, and you were stoned then." Victoria looked at her ring. "The police think you killed her. You're the one who had the bat."

"That wasn't my bat," he whispered. "You're the wolf lady."

"There were a hundred wolf people here that day. I wasn't even dressed up, and you think I'm the one who did it?"

"You *were* dressed up," he said. "Crown and all."

This was getting weird. I stepped in. "Okay, that's enough."

Victoria's head swiveled toward me. "It's about time you got here," she said. "He's talking nonsense again. We'll never solve this murder if he doesn't fess up to what he saw."

Ansel seemed to shrink in on himself the more she yelled.

"You're right, *we* won't solve this murder," I said. "*We* are park rangers. Not police officers. We don't investigate murders."

"Since when?" Victoria rested her hands on her hips.

"Since now," I said. "I've changed, and I won't let you go down the investigation path. At least not while I'm your training officer."

Victoria rolled her eyes so far back in her head she probably saw her ginormous engineering brain.

"Ansel, you know you can't be here," I said. "The police told you that, right?"

"Yeah," Ansel said, hanging his head.

"Come on out of there," I said. "I have to call the police so they can escort you out."

"I'm not coming out until she's gone," he pointed at Victoria.

"Oh my God," Victoria said. "Fine, I'll leave. I'm ready to get home to my fiancé anyway." She smiled down at her ring. "He's only in town one more night."

I could have barfed. She and Troy would be perfect for each other.

"What else needs to be locked up?" she asked.

"The office and the banquet hall."

She didn't even acknowledge me before turning and storming away.

"Let's meet at the truck when you're done," I yelled after her.

I took out my phone, found Bryant's contact information, and hit send.

"She isn't like the other wolf ladies," Ansel said beside me. "She's real."

"They were real too," I said.

"Hello?" Bryant said.

"It's Rylie Cooper. Ansel is back in the park. I thought I'd let you know."

"I'll send someone over right away."

I told him where to have them meet me and hung up.

Ansel was trying to tell me more about the wolf lady—Victoria—but I was purposely blocking him out. Knowing that information would make me want to investigate. "Have you told all of this to the police?"

"Yes," he said. "But they don't believe me."

A text popped up on my phone from Antonio.

Everything okay with your nemesis and the stoner?

I texted back.

Can this day be over already?

His reply made me laugh.

Chin up buttercup, only a week and four days to go.

I shoved my phone back into my pocket.

"She was like the lady off that dragon show, the queen of the dragons, you know?" He stepped out from beneath the slide.

I didn't know what dragon show he was talking about. "So, wolf lady was the queen of the other wolves?"

"Yes." Ansel lit up as if I finally understood his crazy

ramblings. "And I saw her kill that lady. You better be careful. She doesn't seem to like you very much either."

"But, you told all of this to the police, right?"

He sighed. "Yes, I already told you that."

"Good."

We stood in silence for a few minutes before screams erupted from the mic on my shoulder.

"No. Please don't," Victoria's voice was scared.

"Wait here," I said to Ansel before sprinting back toward the offices.

A thudding sound came after the screams and then more screaming.

Someone was attacking Victoria. She must have pushed the red button on the mic that held the channel open in emergencies. At least she'd remembered that part of the radio training.

"Rylie!" She screamed so loudly it echoed off the buildings. "Don't! Rylie!"

Another thud.

"Why are you doing this?" Victoria asked, her voice weak now. "Did you kill Michelle?"

I pulled out my keys and opened the office door.

The person attacking her was silent. Not so much as a footstep between the thuds and Victoria's screams for mercy.

The office was pitch black, and the alarm had been set.

They weren't here.

"Rylie," her voice was soft now. "Please stop."

Then the mic cut out. Silence buzzed in my ears.

I pulled out my asp and held it extended at my side. If someone attacked Victoria, they'd probably attack me too.

"Ranger Seven, Ranger Fourteen?" I called, hopeful. But there was no answer. "Ranger Seven, Ranger Five?"

"I already have rescue and PD heading your way," Antonio said.

"Thank you."

"Be careful," Antonio replied.

"Copy," I said then clicked the mic again. "Ranger Seven, Ranger Fourteen?" I called out as I opened the unlocked door to the banquet hall.

My voice echoed.

She was in here.

I wanted to call out for her, but I didn't want to give away my position in case the person who'd attacked her was still in the room.

I flipped on the lights gripping my baton more tightly in my hand.

The only thing I could see was a bloody and beaten Victoria lying in a heap in the middle of the floor.

I rushed to her side. "Victoria, are you okay?" Aviator sunglasses rested over her eyes. She hadn't worn sunglasses since I'd known her.

The image of Michelle with aviator glasses pinged in my head. This was the same attacker.

I glanced around. The room was empty, but the door to the kitchen was open. Whoever did this probably went out the back door.

"Victoria? Talk to me."

She groaned. I pulled on gloves so I wouldn't mess up any evidence.

A quick check of her duty belt showed that nothing

had been stolen. Victoria hadn't even been able to get her pepper spray out of the holster.

"Hang in there," I said. "The ambulance is coming."

I put my baton down beside me and held her hand.

"Ranger Seven, Ranger Five?"

"Five," Antonio said.

"Please tell the medics we're in the banquet hall."

"Copy."

"Stay with me," I said soothingly. "You're going to be okay."

"Wolf lady," she mumbled. "Crown."

"Wolf lady?" I asked.

"Ansel," she said. "Knows."

Then she lost consciousness.

"Victoria, please." I squeezed her hand. "Troy needs you. Wake up. It's okay. I forgive you. Even if I did hate you, that's all over now. Just don't die."

I looked down at the hand I was squeezing and noticed her ring was gone. Had this been a mugging? And if it was, why did she say Ansel knows?

No.

I slammed on the brakes in my head.

I was not going down the rabbit trail. My job was doing what I had been doing all day—not solving murders. Not that this was a murder. Oh God, she couldn't die.

"Rylie?" A voice came from the doorway.

I snatched up my baton and stood to my feet in one fluid motion.

"It's okay. It's the paramedics."

I dropped the baton down to my side. "She's right

here." I moved aside so they could see her. "Please help her."

They went about doing their jobs as I looked on.

"She was talking a few seconds ago," I said. "Then she passed out."

"What did she say when she was talking?" Detective Bryant asked from behind me.

"I thought you were sending someone else."

"I was until I heard there was another assault at the reservoir." He glanced down at my baton. It was covered in blood from lying next to Victoria. "I don't think I've ever driven that fast in my life."

"The attacker got away. Again."

"Again?" Bryant asked.

"She said wolf lady, crown, and that Ansel knows." I pointed to Victoria. "Plus, both Victoria and Michelle—the woman from the other day—had aviator sunglasses perfectly placed on their faces. I don't know about Michelle, but I've never seen Victoria wear or even carry any sunglasses with her."

He pulled on gloves and put the glasses—which the paramedics had removed—into an evidence bag.

He looked at my baton again. "Did you hit someone with that?"

"No, I set it down next to Victoria."

He nodded. "Did you see anyone?"

"They probably went out the back." I pointed to the open door leading to the kitchen. "I haven't seen anyone other than Ansel down here for at least an hour."

Detective Bryant glanced down at the phone in his hand. "Who has apparently fled the scene."

Damn. "I had to leave him," I said. "I couldn't stay with him while Victoria was being attacked."

"You did the right thing." He sighed. "I'm going to need you to come down to the station and give a statement."

"Tonight?"

"Tonight. You can ride with me."

Fun . . . not.

"How will I get Cherry Anne?"

"I'll bring you back," he said.

So much for my top-down decompressing drive home.

"But the drive is so far. It'll be two in the morning before I get home, and I have to work tomorrow." A weight dropped in my stomach. I'd be working tomorrow without Victoria. Victoria was probably not coming back to the reservoir. Ever.

I may have wanted her gone, but not like this.

Another weight dropped in my stomach.

Ursula was going to kill me.

"Fine, you can drive yourself. But no dilly-dallying. I want to get home tonight too." Bryant moved to talk to the other officers who had just walked through the door.

The paramedics lifted the stretcher with Victoria on it and hurried to the ambulance.

I squeezed her hand briefly as they walked by. "You'll be okay. Be strong."

It was funny—well, not funny—but interesting how you could start a day hoping someone would eject themselves from your life and end a day wishing they wouldn't have.

I followed Bryant to the police station, feeling guilty I'd ever thought Victoria had hurt Michelle. Just because I hated her didn't mean she was capable of murder. Another reason I'd be a terrible cop—I let my emotions overrun my investigative abilities.

I made sure to chuck my aviator glasses out the window the minute I hit the highway. I'd never wear a pair like them again.

I'd visited Luke a couple of times at this station, but the place felt cold and intimidating without him.

"Let's start from the beginning," Bryant said when we were seated across from each other in the same interrogation room I'd been questioned in not long before.

Even when I tried to stay out of things, they seemed to follow me.

"Victoria and I were closing up. I had her go down to the bathrooms to lock them while I locked the offices. But she called me over before I could set the alarm."

"She called you over where?"

"To the playground. She found Ansel. He was screaming at her about being the wolf lady." I sighed. "Obviously, he was wrong."

Bryant nodded. "Keep going."

"Then I called you, and Victoria went to lock up the office and the banquet hall." I left out the part about getting home to her fiancé—my ex-boyfriend. "I waited with Ansel until I heard her screaming over the radio."

"Before you heard her screaming, did Ansel tell you anything?"

"I didn't ask, and I tried not to listen. Trust me, I've taken the don't investigate message to heart."

"That's not why I was asking, but okay."

"I do remember him saying the wolf lady wasn't like the other wolf ladies. She was like the queen of the—uh —" I couldn't remember what he'd said. "It's from a tv show or something."

"Dragons?"

"Yeah. Dragons." He wasn't taking notes, but the conversation was probably being recorded. Luke would have been taking notes. "But he said he'd already told you all of this."

"He did," Bryant said. "What happened when you heard her screaming?"

"I told Ansel to stay put—which he obviously didn't— and ran toward the office. I should have gone straight to the banquet hall. Maybe then I'd have at least seen who attacked her."

"You didn't know where she was." Bryant tried to comfort me. "You had a fifty-fifty shot."

"Yeah," I said. "So I went to the office instead of the

banquet hall and when I unlocked it, the alarm had already been set. Oh, shit." I lowered my head into my hands. I'd forgotten to disarm the building.

"What?"

"The alarm would have gone off if I didn't disarm and reset it." I looked up at him. "The security company probably called Ben and woke up his whole family."

"It's been taken care of," Bryant said. "I believe Antonio got it situated."

That was a relief. "Where was I?"

"You went into the office."

"I left the office when I realized my mistake and ran over to the banquet hall where the door was unlocked." I tried to remember everything that happened. "I called out on my radio and heard my voice echo, so I knew she was inside even though the lights were off. I pulled out my baton and turned on the lights, but the only one there was Victoria."

"And she was conscious?"

"Barely."

"Remind me what she said."

"She said wolf lady, crown, and Ansel knows. That's it. Do you think a wolf lady is going around beating up women?"

"I'd rather not speculate," Bryant said. "If she wasn't coherent, she may have been transferring the conversation she had with Ansel onto the situation." He sat back in his chair. "Is there anything else you'd like to tell me?"

I considered telling him about Victoria's and my history, but that was irrelevant to this case.

"Victoria knew the woman who died—Michelle."

Bryant's eyes narrowed. "How do you know?"

"She told me today. I guess they dated the same guy a long time ago and they became friends. She said it was a keep your enemies closer situation."

Bryant said nothing but looked toward the door. "Is that it?"

"Her engagement ring was stolen," I said. "She just got engaged and had been flaunting the ring all day. It was massive."

"Do you know the name of her fiancé?"

"I think it was Troy," I said. "Not sure, though. It could have been Trey or Tom, maybe." I couldn't let on that I knew for a fact it *was* Troy and that he was a lying cheating piece of—

"Anything else?"

I sucked in a breath. "Do you know if Victoria is okay?"

"She's in surgery," Bryant said. "Probably will be for several hours."

Michelle had died in surgery. My stomach twisted. "Can I go now?"

"Let me make sure we don't have any other questions," he said before leaving the room.

My entire body felt numb. A couple of hours ago, I was talking to Victoria, and now, she was on the brink of death.

The door opened, and Bryant peeked his head in. "You're free to go."

I wiped the tears that had gathered in my eyes with the sleeve of my hoodie.

"If you think of anything else, let us know," he said.

When I walked out into the lobby, Antonio was walking through the front doors.

"Are you here to give them your statement?" I asked.

"They heard everything I did," he said. "I wanted to make sure you were okay."

He opened his arms, and I fell into them, letting the tears flow. "I may have hated her, but I didn't want anything bad like this to happen."

"Shhh," he whispered. "You should not admit you hated someone who was just assaulted. Especially in a police station."

"I should have been there for her. Why did I let her lock up alone?" I let out a sob. "I should have gone straight to the banquet hall. If I had, I might have been able to catch whoever did this."

He squeezed me tighter. "You did everything right."

"I didn't see anyone down there. Not a single person. What if I was their target? I need to be more observant."

"Shhh. It will be okay. It was a coincidence."

He laid his head on top of mine and ran a hand down my hair. I could feel a blush travel up my neck into my cheeks.

I pulled away. I shouldn't have been hugging him. The last time we were this close, we'd kissed, and it nearly cost me my relationship with Garrett.

"Thanks for checking up on me. And for figuring out the alarm stuff." I took a step back. "I should probably go home now."

He nodded as if he understood. "I'm glad you are okay."

"I just hope Victoria is too."

The entire ranger staff, minus the trail rangers who stayed at the reservoirs, went to the hospital the next day.

I stayed toward the back of the pack for two reasons. One, I felt responsible for Victoria's attack. And two, because Troy would probably be there, and as much as I'd wrestled with it all night, I still hadn't come to terms with seeing him.

Victoria was hooked up to a slew of monitors and had bandages all over her body that made my road rash bandages look like Barbie Band-Aids.

"Thank you so much for coming." A woman who I assumed to be Victoria's mother accepted the large bouquet we'd all pitched in for from Greg. "I'm sure Victoria would feel so special knowing you all made the trip."

I gingerly peeked out from behind everyone, but the only person there was her mom. I let out a sigh of relief. I'd live to face my fears another day.

"Are you Rylie?" her mother asked Nikki.

"No, Rylie's—" Nikki looked around to find me "—right there."

Before I knew it, Victoria's mother had her arms wrapped around my neck.

"Thank you so much for saving my baby. If you hadn't been there, she probably would have died."

"She was a smart girl," I said. "She pressed the emergency button, which connected her directly to dispatch. If I hadn't been there, someone would have."

"Victoria said you were modest." Her mother released me. "If there's anything I can do for you, please let me know."

"Thank you."

We didn't stay long. Victoria's mother looked exhausted.

"Do you need anything before we go?" Greg asked.

"Ursula should be here soon to sit with her. I'll be okay until then," she said. "But thank you."

We said our goodbyes, and I brought up the rear again.

Just as we were about to get on the elevator, Ursula stepped out. "Rylie, I need to talk to you."

The other rangers raised their eyebrows as they loaded the elevator. Nikki shrugged and mouthed an apology before the doors closed.

Ursula looked around, then pulled me to the side of the hallway. "I need you to investigate this attack."

"But you said—"

"Someone tried to kill the person I love most in this world."

"But the police—"

"Victoria trusted you. She adored you."

Did she? Or had she just said that to keep her enemies closer?

"You have a certain way of figuring things out," Ursula said. "The police are spinning in circles, and when they realize they have nothing, they'll drop this case to move onto something bigger."

"But what about Detective Bryant?"

"What about Harry Bryant?"

"He warned me not to investigate. He *arrested* me last time. I do not want to go to jail for sticking my nose into this."

"You have my word. I'll protect you from Harry and any other police officers that try to get in your way." She lowered her voice. "I control all the recreation in this city. If they want to work out, golf, or fish, they have to go through me."

She was scary. I wouldn't want to mess with her.

"Whoever did this is dangerous," I said. "I also promised my fiancé I would stay safe. What if I'm attacked next?"

"Victoria wasn't very street-smart." She glanced down the hall toward Victoria's room. "But you are. You know when you're getting in too deep. Just don't go too far."

Easy for her to say.

"I don't know. It doesn't seem right. I've worked so hard to stay out of it."

"I don't want to have to threaten your job."

"Then don't," I said. "Because I'm tired of being bullied into doing what you want me to do." I'd had enough. I loved being a ranger, and I needed the income, but I was sick of her trying to fire me at every turn.

"You're right. I'm sorry." Her eyes misted over. "I won't threaten your job again."

My thoughts were all over the place. I wanted to jump into the investigation. But it would be so different without Luke there to bounce ideas off of. Plus, I'd already made an enormous mess of the situation. Thinking Victoria was the attacker and then going to the office before the banquet hall. I was not cut out for this stuff.

But Ursula had never looked so sad. I couldn't just tell her no.

"I'll see what I can do," I said. "No promises, though."

Ursula tried to smile. "Thank you."

"Don't thank me yet." I pushed the button for the elevator, and the doors popped open. "Call me when Victoria wakes up. I want to talk to her."

Ursula nodded and walked down the hall.

Standing up for myself should have felt good—empowering. Ursula wouldn't threaten my job anymore. So why did I feel like I was about to vomit?

I took deep breaths all the way down to the ground floor. My stomach seemed to have settled until I saw him.

Troy.

Standing there in all his handsome cheater jerk-face glory—buzzed dirty-blond hair, aviators resting on top of his head, five o'clock shadow, and a surprised smile directed right at me.

Before I could get out a hello, I barfed.

All over him.

"What the hell!" He threw his arms in the air, the smile gone, the flowers in his hand flying across the lobby. "It's nice to see you too. I guess I deserved that."

"What are you doing here?" I asked. "Never mind. I know what you're doing here."

I wiped my mouth with my sleeve.

Everyone in the lobby stared at us.

"How is she?" he asked.

"Unconscious, but they said she should be okay."

"That's good," he said. "Look, about how things ended."

I held up a hand. "Don't. I don't want to hear it. I know you were seeing Victoria longer than you said. I know you cheated on me longer than I realized. I don't need you to make me feel like any more of an idiot than I already do. Plus—" I held up my left hand "—I'm engaged. So I guess we both get to live happily ever after."

"You're engaged." A strange look flashing over his face.

"Yep," I said. "Happily." I pushed past him.

"Rylie, wait."

But I wasn't turning around. I'd said my piece. And now I was going to work.

I waited my entire shift for Ansel to show up again, but I never saw him. The only people I saw were Bella and Shayla rollerblading and pushing their babies and a couple people with their dogs.

"We should close up the offices together tonight, just in case," Ben said.

Typically, I would have brushed him off. Told him I was okay. But I'll admit, I was spooked.

Nothing happened with Ben around, and I was home early enough to have dinner with Shayla, Seamus, and Garrett.

"How are you doing?" Shayla asked. "I hear it was pretty gruesome."

"It was horrible. It looked like someone took a fire poker and beat the living daylights out of her. And to listen to her scream over the radio, not knowing where she was—" I couldn't even complete the sentence. I wrapped my arms around my mid-section. Garrett rubbed my shoulder.

"And Ansel took off?" Seamus asked.

"Wouldn't you?" I asked. "That guy was in the wrong

place at the wrong time. He didn't kill anyone. Heck, he was with me when Victoria started screaming."

"I know it's selfish," Garrett said. "But I'm so glad it wasn't you. I don't know what I'd do if I were visiting you in the hospital right now."

"Speaking of fiancés visiting the hospital. I saw Troy today." I poked at the Mexican takeout in front of me.

"Troy as in—" Garrett started.

"My ex-boyfriend. Victoria's fiancé."

"Fiancé? When did that happen?" Shayla asked.

"The night before last," I said. "She came into work yesterday, flashing her ginormous diamond in everyone's faces."

"That's right, the ring was stolen, wasn't it?" Shayla asked.

"She was wearing it before she went to lock up, but when I found her, it was gone," I said.

"Maybe someone just wanted the ring, and she fought back?" Garrett said.

"That's not what it sounded like on the radio. She kept asking the attacker why they were hitting her. She was calling for me. I tried to get there as soon as I could. If I had been a tiny bit earlier—"

"You could be in a hospital bed next to her," Shayla said. "Don't second guess yourself. It won't change anything."

"Was the other woman missing anything?" I glanced down at the engagement ring on my finger.

Shayla quirked an eyebrow up at me. "You know I can't tell you that. Plus, I thought you weren't investigating this one."

"Sorry, habit," I said. "But maybe if she was wearing a ring too, there would at least be a motive."

"Maybe to be on the safe side, you should leave your ring at home until we—*the police*—find the attacker." Shayla winked.

That meant the other woman had gotten her ring stolen too. Interesting.

"Should I be worried about you going to work?" Garrett asked.

"They've doubled us up on shifts," I said. "No one works alone anymore."

"That's good. Not that I don't trust you to handle yourself, but I worry." Garrett squeezed my hand.

Guilt surged through me at the thought of going behind his back to investigate the case. But I wasn't investigating. Not yet, anyway. Plus, I wouldn't let myself get in too deep. I'd be fine. And I owed it to Victoria to find out who did this to her.

"What do you think about December seventh?" Garrett asked when we'd settled into my bed for the night.

"December seventh, for what?" I laid on my right side —the small spoon—and Garrett curled around me, his head resting in the crook of my neck.

"For the wedding," he said. "Your mom mentioned how much you've talked about a winter wedding."

My heart paused in my chest. I'd talked about a winter wedding when Luke and I were together.

In high school.

I'd never considered marrying anyone else in the winter.

Not even Troy.

"Or we can do another date," Garrett said. "I thought if we did it before the end of the year, we could claim married on our taxes for the entire year."

Says the accountant.

So romantic.

"December." My voice came out squeaky. I cleared my throat. "December seventh is perfect."

He squeezed me with his big arms and kissed my neck, sending shivers down my spine.

I giggled and turned toward him.

"Since we're discussing it, what do you think about colors?" Garrett asked.

I kissed him. "How about pink and black?"

"Pink and black sound very classy."

"And roses for the flowers?" I asked.

"Pink roses?"

"And maybe white," I said. "To offset."

"Beautiful."

"Should we write our own vows?"

"I'm not much of a writer," he said.

"Me neither." I wrinkled my nose. "Let's go traditional."

"I'm good with that."

"What about locations?" I asked.

"We could find somewhere in the city. Or the mountains if you wanted to do it up there."

"I'd love a mountain wedding. Maybe even at the top of a ski slope."

"I don't ski," he said.

"You've never been skiing?"

He shook his head.

"Snowboarding?"

"Nope."

"I could teach you."

"I've never really been into the whole winter sports scene." He gave me an apologetic smile. "But we could do it on a ski slope and come back down on the chairlift."

That sounded boring, but I knew I'd have to compromise on some things. "Let's think about it," I said. "If we did, maybe we could have the reception in the ski lodge."

"How many people are we inviting?" he asked.

"I think we could keep it pretty small, don't you? Family and close friends?"

"It'll keep the cost down."

"I don't think my parents are worried about the cost," I said.

"I'd like to help pay for the wedding if they'll allow it." He ran a hand up my arm. "I've never liked the tradition that the bride's parents have to pay for everything."

"I can talk to them about it," I said, knowing they'd likely refuse his money.

"I can't wait to marry you," Garrett said, kissing me so passionately my toes curled.

I couldn't wait to marry him either.

14

After not seeing Ansel for three more days, I decided to use my day off to track him down. Ursula was only too happy to get me his home address if it meant I was trying to find her niece's attacker.

Victoria still hadn't come out of her coma, and Ursula was getting antsy.

I had to double-check the address three times before I gathered the courage to ring the doorbell. Ansel's house was in a very ritzy neighborhood.

The doorbell sounded like an old grandfather clock, and a butler answered.

A butler.

Ansel—the dreadlocked stoner under the slide—had a freaking butler. Maybe he was a drug dealer. Or maybe he lived with his parents.

"Hi," I said. "I'm here to see Ansel."

The butler looked me up and down, obviously judging my choice of ripped jeans, flip-flops, and a white tank.

"Ansel has already spoken to numerous police officers, and he's not speaking to the press."

"I'm neither," I said. "I'm a park ranger at Alder Ridge Reservoir. I hadn't seen him there for a few days and wanted to make sure he was okay."

"What is your name?"

"Rylie Cooper."

"Please wait here." The butler closed the door, leaving me on the front step like a vacuum salesman.

I took in the house again. It had to have at least six bedrooms. It was one of those houses that probably had more bathrooms than bedrooms.

"Rylie," Ansel appeared at the door wearing an ironed pair of blue jeans and a black polo. But the most startling part of his appearance wasn't his sleek attire. It was his shaved head. Without the dreadlocks, he was almost entirely unrecognizable. "Please come in."

He led me through a beautiful foyer to a sunken living room that looked just like the one from the Brady Bunch, only more expensive.

"This is amazing," I said. "I loved the Brady Bunch."

"I did as well," Ansel said, his words and his posture confident. He was so much different when he wasn't stoned. "Please sit."

We sat on retro couches, and the butler brought us each a lemonade.

"Thank you." I sipped the tart drink, unable to take my eyes off Ansel's changed appearance.

"I think I know why you're here." Ansel crossed one leg over the other, his ankle resting on his knee, with an arm draped over the back of the couch.

"You do?"

"I have done nothing but cause stress for you and your colleagues. Please accept my apology."

He thought I was here to get an apology?

"I assure you," he continued, "I will not get high again."

"I'm here to talk to you about what you saw the other night," I said. "And see if you'd remembered anything from the attack you witnessed."

"I'm afraid I don't remember much. Part of the reason I'm not going to get high any longer is because it has been affecting my short-term memory. The board of my company has threatened to boot me if I can't get my act together."

I so badly wanted to ask what his company did but thought better of it. That wasn't why I was here.

"Anything you remember might help. You talked about the wolf lady or dragon lady. Does that ring a bell?"

Ansel shook his head almost as if he was embarrassed. "I'm sure I said a lot of things. But just as the police have concluded, nothing I said under the influence is to be trusted."

I was getting frustrated. It was almost as if he was *trying* to hide information.

Could he have been part of all this? Maybe he was a decoy for the person who attacked Michelle and Victoria.

"Did you know Michelle or Victoria?" I asked.

"I can't say that I did. I don't mean to be unhelpful, but I don't recall anything about the attacks."

This was getting me nowhere. I stood. "I won't keep

you any longer," I said. "If you think of anything, you can call me at the reservoir."

"I will most certainly do that," he said as he escorted me back out the door. "And please pass along my apologies to the other rangers."

I nodded and headed back to Cherry Anne. Something wasn't right about him, but I couldn't put my finger on it.

My only other lead was what Ansel had said when he was high—the wolf lady. The most logical place to start was the event—hundreds of women dressed as wolves that day. But how many of them had been wearing a crown?

I pulled up Instagram and searched for the author. Under her newest release was a whole slew of hashtags. One was #teamwerewolf. I clicked and scrolled through the photos searching for anyone who looked like the queen of the wolves.

When I came across a photo of a group of werewolf-people, I clicked on the profile that posted the picture. I did a mental head slap. The profile was none other than Logan Labrec's. She had photos. Lots of photos. She said she always took way too many.

I picked up my cell and tapped on her name.

"Logan," she said, answering on the second ring.

"Hey, it's Rylie Cooper."

"What's up?"

"I was just scrolling through Instagram and saw some of your photos from the event at the reservoir last weekend."

"I got some good ones, huh?"

"You did," I said. "I wanted to know if I could see the other photos and videos you took that day. I'm looking into the woman's death, and I thought you might have caught something with your camera."

"Wouldn't that be something?" she said. "Yeah, sure. How about tonight? You can come over to our place?"

I hadn't been to Eli Hudson's new house. I would have been lying if I said I wasn't excited. "Sounds good. I'll bring pizza."

"Meat-lovers for me," she said.

"A girl after my own heart."

I punched my guest code into the box and waited for the gates to open. Eli and Logan's home was the stuff dreams were made of.

The large wooden gate retracted into the stone wall, revealing a mansion. Five peaks of varying heights with huge windows mimicked its pristine view of the mountains. Mature trees were carefully disbursed to look natural though I expected they had been very precisely placed. A stone fountain sat directly in the center of the circular driveway that snaked around the side of the house to where I suspected was a large garage.

I didn't get that far. A valet stopped me as I approached the front door and insisted on parking my car. I resisted the urge to give Cherry Anne a goodbye pat.

Logan waited at the front door dressed in a casual pair of jeans I suspected cost more than my monthly rent and a tank top with the name of a local band on the front. Her brown hair was straight and shiny.

"Come in," Logan said as I walked through the arched doorway into a foyer with a chandelier hanging from the ceiling. Two sets of stairs led to the second level, and an archway on each side lead to other well-lit rooms. "Can I get you anything to drink?"

I handed her the pizza box. "Bud Light?"

"Lime?" she asked.

"Sure."

She walked into the kitchen and set the pizza box next to a couple of neatly stacked paper plates. A beer tap with the Bud Light logo on it came out of the countertop along with a few others I didn't recognize. She expertly poured us two glasses and added a lime to the rim.

I was too in awe to say anything. The kitchen was the most exquisite one I'd ever seen.

"Shall we?" she asked.

I grabbed the box and the plates and followed her through a sparsely furnished room with high ceilings and a fireplace that nearly took up an entire wall. On the other side of the room was what might have been a small dining room—octagonal with windows on every wall looking out toward the in-ground pool—but was Logan's office.

"Your house is gorgeous," I said, finally finding my words.

We sat at her superbly organized desk situated directly in the center of the room, where a dining room table would have gone.

"It's not my house," she said. "Though I had a big

hand in finding it and decorating. So thanks." She shrugged.

We dug into the pizza and beer. "I appreciate your help with all of this." I took a bite of the meaty deliciousness.

"Any time." She took a daintier bite and wiped her mouth as she chewed. "Eli said you had a thing for investigation. It definitely piqued my interest."

"It's not as fun as it may sound."

She smiled in a way that seemed to call my bluff.

"Okay, maybe it is kind of fun," I admitted. "But don't tell anyone I told you that."

"Why not?" she asked.

"It seems like I'm the only person who thinks me investigating crimes is a good idea. Well, except for Ursula, who only wants me to because it's her niece who's in the hospital right now."

"Don't listen to them. If it's what you want to do, then do it."

"I could lose my job, my friends, my fiancé, and maybe even go to jail."

"Eli said you don't want to be a cop because they carry guns, right?" She seemed to be enjoying the pizza and beer as much as I was.

"Basically."

"Then become a private investigator. They investigate things all the time and don't go to jail." She folded her napkin neatly on her lap. "And if your friends and fiancé can't support your dreams, find new ones."

Easy for her to say. Eli was probably the most supportive boyfriend in the entire universe. Logan could do anything, and he'd practically bow down to her.

"Speaking of life changes, what happened to your job? Why did you get benched?"

Logan sighed. "I may have said something about one of the opposing team's coaches that was completely true, yet rather unprofessional."

"Did the coach overhear you?"

"He did," she said. "Everyone did. I didn't know my mic was hot. It was a national television program."

"Shit," I said.

She was silent.

"At least you weren't fired completely, right?"

"If my father wasn't the head of the network, I would have been." Her face didn't give away any of her emotions. "I always said I'd do it without my father's help. But if I didn't, I'd be completely out of a job."

"So now you're stuck doing book signings instead of NFL games?"

"Basically," she said. "Until I can prove my worth again. At least this time, I'll know when I get the promotion that I got it on my own merit. Even Daddy can't completely save me on this one."

I could appreciate wanting to work your way up on your own merits.

"But that's enough about that," she said. "Let's get going with the photos." Logan opened her laptop and scrolled through rows and rows of specifically labeled folders to the one with photos from the event. "I looked through them but didn't see anything suspicious."

As we searched through endless pictures and watched videos of the hoards of people at the author event, we finished off the large pizza.

"You know, Eli told me he gave you his number when he met you."

I laughed. "I think he was mistaken. He didn't give me his number."

"On your jersey? He said he signed it and put his number on it." She scrolled through more photos—ones of the regulars: the runners, dog walkers, fishermen, and baby pushers. "But you didn't call, so your loss."

This woman had more confidence than any person I had ever met.

"I think things worked out just fine," I said, but my mind reeled with the thought that Eli Hudson had been interested in me.

I mean, I knew we had a spark, but he actually gave me his number? How had I never seen it on my jersey?

Probably because the day I'd gotten it signed was the day Garrett and I had a fantastic day together, only to have Luke arrest him and haul him off to jail.

"Ooh, stop there," I said. "Can you zoom in on that one?"

A group of werewolf-people stood in one corner of the photograph.

"Does it look like they're all focused on her?" I pointed to a woman who stood toward the right of the screen. I couldn't see her face, but every single one of the other werewolf-people watched her.

"Yeah," Logan said. "That's weird."

"Can we look at other pictures with her in them?"

She was unmistakable in a deep purple robe, a crown, and a long blonde braid trailing down her back. She might have looked a little bit like Victoria. Especially to someone who was high.

Logan scrolled through more pictures, and each time we saw the purple-robbed werewolf, she would stop and zoom in. And in every image, the surrounding people fixated on her.

"Wait," I said. "Stop there."

Logan gasped when she zoomed in. "Is that—"

"Her name is Michelle," I said. "And it looks like she's at odds with the werewolf queen."

I scanned the photo more closely. Michelle wasn't wearing sunglasses. And I could almost see a ring on her left hand.

"Could you send me that picture?" I asked. "And maybe one that shows the werewolf lady's face?"

"Are you going to run it through facial recognition?" Logan asked.

"I don't have that ability," I said. "But the police might. You don't mind if I show the police, do you?"

"Not at all." She pulled up a video. "But maybe you should talk to the author first. Listen to this."

The video was of Logan and the author sitting down for a chat. There weren't many people around, and the sun was setting, meaning it was probably after the signing had concluded.

"How does it make you feel when you see all these people dressing up as characters from your books standing in huge lines waiting for a chance to meet you?"

"It feels great. It's the reason I write." A canned answer if I'd ever heard one.

"Okay, but really," Logan pushed. "It has to be strange to see your books come to life."

"If my books came to life, there would be a lot more blood and gore," she said with a laugh, then paled. "Oh, I'm sorry. Can you leave out that part? I forgot about that woman." She dropped her head into her hands. "Sometimes, I can be so dense."

"Sure, I'll leave it out," Logan said. "Your books are pretty brutal. Do you think that could have had something to do with what happened today?"

I looked at Logan, impressed. She had a knack for interviewing people.

"Honestly, I don't know. I hope not. But I wouldn't put it past some of these people." She dropped her voice to a whisper. "They're a little much if you ask me."

"What do you mean by much?"

"They just get so into it. Like, I never thought the books would get this popular. They were always so much fun to write, but they were supposed to be fiction. Then people started dressing up and acting them out."

"That sounds like it could be scary," Logan said. "Do your fans ever freak you out or make you feel unsafe?"

"Not really," the author said. "But they do steal things."

"What kind of things?"

"Books mostly. We keep an inventory of how many we sell, but every time we end up short."

"Maybe it's the staff?" Logan asked.

"Could be." The author shrugged. "But then one time, our bus got broken into, and someone stole all of my socks and my jewelry."

My ears perked up at the mention of jewelry.

"Did you report it to the police?" Logan asked on the video.

"I did," the author said. "But nothing came of it. I submitted an insurance claim, and they paid me for the estimated value, but how do you estimate value on priceless earrings, necklaces, and rings?"

"Stop there," I said.

Logan paused the video. "Does that mean something to you?"

"It might," I said. "Does she say anything else about the jewelry?"

"No, but let me fast forward a bit. These next few minutes, she freaks out because she realizes I've been recording the entire conversation. I have to assure her several times that I won't go public with the video."

She stops at a place where the author looks like she's about in tears. "It would ruin my career," she said. "My publicist would be furious with me."

"Don't worry. I won't let it leak." Logan replied on the video.

"Here," Logan, sitting next to me, said. "Watch this."

She pointed at the background.

"Is that the werewolf in the purple cape?" I asked.

The werewolf was waving to the author, her entourage following closely behind.

"See that one?" the author says almost at a whisper. "She's one of the every-eventers. She's the leader of one of my fan clubs."

Logan paused it again. "Looks like you need to find this fan club."

15

Before I could go any further with the investigation, I had to see something for myself. I found it in the back of my closet.

The jersey.

And sure enough, it had Eli Hudson's phone number scrawled below his signature.

"Why do you look like you just found a rat in your hamper?" Shayla's voice startled me so much I dropped the jersey to the floor.

I quickly reached down and picked it up, returning it to its hanger. "No reason."

"Is that your Eli jersey?"

I laughed. "Yeah. When I saw Logan, she told me Eli had given me his number. I had to see for myself."

"Eli gave you his number?" She wiggled her eyebrows. "I wondered if he liked you."

"We flirted a bit, but I didn't think he liked me as in wanted to date me." Though there had been that time when I'd had a mini-accidental-date with one of his team-mates, and he said Eli talked about me.

Shayla leaned against the door frame. "How do you think your life would be different right now if you'd chosen him over Garrett?"

"I'd probably live in a mansion," I said. "You should see his house."

"You went to his house?"

"To see Logan," I said. "And everything turned out just the way it should have. Eli and Logan are perfect together."

"As are you and Garrett, right?" Shayla prompted.

"Right," I said. "Of course. That's a given." I put the jersey back in the closet and closed the door. "Speaking of, I need to ask you a question."

"Yes?" Shayla batted her eyelashes at me. She likely knew what I was going to ask her.

"Will you be one of my bridesmaids?"

Shayla practically jumped into my arms. "Yes! I will absolutely be a bridesmaid." She squeezed my neck so hard I thought my head might pop off. "Does that mean you have a date?"

"December seventh," I said. "And maybe even in the mountains."

She flopped onto my bed. "How romantic."

"Do you think you and Seamus will get married in Ireland?" I asked.

"Seamus and I are not getting married." Shayla waved her left hand in my face.

I swatted her hand away. "Not yet."

Shayla rolled toward me, propping her head up on her hand. "What were you doing at Logan's anyway?"

I considered lying, but if Ursula had a chat with Detective Bryant, it was only a matter of time before Shayla knew I was looking into the assault. "Don't be mad, okay?"

Shayla closed her eyes as if she was trying to gather her patience. She'd make a great mom someday.

"Ursula asked me to help with the investigation."

"And you said yes?" Her voice wasn't angry. It was more of a whisper, which made it more terrifying than if she had flat out yelled at me.

"I didn't say no."

"If she threatened your job—"

"She did," I interrupted. "But I shut her down. I told her she couldn't keep manipulating me that way."

Shayla opened her eyes. "Good."

"And I'm not investigating anything real. Not yet, anyway."

"Does Garrett know?"

I shook my head. "You know how he worries."

"For good reason."

"I know," I said. "But this time is different. I'm not going to put myself in harm's way. I'm going to be extra super careful. Pinky promise."

She took my pinky in her own and shook it twice. "Don't you think Detective Bryant will try to arrest you again?"

"Apparently, Ursula has the upper hand in that relationship. Whatever she says, goes."

Shayla nodded as if she knew exactly what I was

talking about. "If you're going to do this, I think you should work with someone in the department."

"Bryant?" I asked.

"No," she said. "Not Detective Bryant. Maybe Jerry."

"Jerry hates me." Jerry was Luke's partner when Luke had been on the department.

"Jerry doesn't hate you." Shayla sighed. "I think he might actually like you."

That was a stretch, and we both knew it.

"Either way," she continued. "Jerry can process any information you get and pass it along to where it needs to go."

"I can probably do that."

"Not probably."

"Okay, fine. I'll do that." Right after I figured out what the deal was with the wolf lady.

"Anything you want to share right now? Did Logan have a lead? I could pass it along to Jerry?"

"Not really. I just wanted to go through the event footage," I said. "See if there was anything to the wolf lady comments Ansel made."

"And?"

"There were a lot of wolf ladies at that event," I said. "In other shocking news, Ansel is a millionaire."

"Ansel? As in the stoner from the playground?"

"Yep," I said. "You should have seen his house. And his butler. And his shaved head."

"I didn't know people had butlers anymore."

I nodded. "And he was dressed in super expensive clothes and talked like a millionaire."

Shayla laughed. "Did he have any information?"

"He said he has short-term memory loss," I said. "But I don't believe it. There's more to the story, but I can't figure out what."

"He acted weird when he was in custody," Shayla said. "He accused every female who walked through the jail of being the wolf lady."

"He thought Victoria was too," I said.

"Any word on her condition?"

"Still unconscious," I said. "I haven't gotten the guts up to go back and visit her. I don't want to run into Troy."

"Maybe we could go together," Shayla said. "I wouldn't mind meeting this infamous Troy."

"He's nothing to write home about."

"And yet, you still don't seem to have forgiven him." Shayla stood up from my bed.

"Why should I?" I huffed. "He's a tool and a half. He doesn't deserve my forgiveness."

"Forgiveness isn't for the person you're forgiving. It's for you. You stewing about how he wronged you isn't hurting him. He obviously couldn't care less."

Her words stung. Because as much as I didn't ever want to be with Troy again, it sucked to know he held so little regard for me after we were together for so long. "I'll work on it."

Shayla gave me a little hug. "You got a good one in Garrett," she said. "Don't let your anger toward your past mess up your future happiness."

I thought about it. Troy hadn't asked for my forgiveness. And even if he had, he didn't deserve it. Shayla was usually pretty insightful about these things, but this time I wasn't so sure.

When Shayla left, I searched for the author's fan club. There were multiple fan clubs—one for each of the creatures within the books. I clicked on the werewolf club, and a woman with long blonde hair and a pretty smile appeared on the first page. Her name was Becky Fredrickson, and from her profile on Facebook, it looked like she lived in the Denver Metro area.

Her Instagram feed included photos of pictures from books events tagged in locations all over the country. She was always in costume complete with the purple robe and crown, and in nine images out of ten, she had an entourage surrounding her.

The next author event was at the Big Mountain Lodge and Resort in my hometown next weekend. If I couldn't track her down beforehand, I'd be sure to make an appearance at that event.

"How you doing, girlie?" Carmen, the big-boobed, big-haired receptionist, gave me her megawatt smile when I walked into the park office.

"I'm doing," I said. "You?"

Carmen blew a bubble with her bubble gum and let it pop on her lips. She laughed and used a long fingernail to put it all back into her mouth. "No complaints here."

"That's good."

"Well, other than the new summies."

My ears perked up. "What do you mean?"

"There's just something weird about them. I've been here a long time, and I've never seen summies that are so well-equipped."

"I think Ursula hired them to look after me. To make sure I was staying in line and staying out of investigations." I chuckled. So much for that plan.

"But you're going to look into this, right? I mean,

you're not going to let whoever did this to Victoria and that other woman get away."

I shrugged. I didn't want to give away that I was looking into it.

"Either way, you better keep your eyes peeled for those summies. They're trouble, I know it."

I had no reason not to trust her.

"Are you talking about the summies?" Antonio asked, popping his head out from the back office.

"Don't you think they're weird?" Carmen blew another bubble and giggled when it covered her nose this time.

Antonio laughed along with her. "Weird is one word." Antonio smiled at me. "Suspicious is probably a better word. They ask a lot of questions."

"What kind of questions?" I asked.

"About the people who work here." He glanced from Carmen to me and back again.

"See, I told ya," Carmen said. "They're trouble."

"Have you figured out anything about Sondra yet?" I asked.

"She is completely shut off. Does not want to be friends. Does not want to share personal details." Antonio rubbed a hand through his luscious brown hair and sighed. "At least Tatiana is nice to Ben. She has some wicked stories about her time as a Florida ranger. She wrestled an alligator."

I tried to imagine Tatiana with her half-shaved head wrestling an alligator. It seemed possible.

"Are you and I closing together tonight?" I asked.

Antonio nodded. "I have been instructed to keep you

safe. Especially since you are probably next in line."

A shiver ran down my spine. "Next in line? What do you mean?"

Antonio glanced at Carmen, who didn't look up from her keyboard—intentionally ignoring us, but most certainly hanging onto every word we said.

"Victoria was attacked where you were supposed to be. And this guy has a type."

"Guy? Why would you think it's a guy?" I asked. I hadn't even considered the possibility of it being a guy. Probably because Ansel called the person a wolf *lady*. Maybe I was taking too much stock in what Ansel said.

"It just seems brutal for a woman to beat another woman so viciously without a motive."

"Maybe there was a motive." An idea dawned on me. What if it wasn't a wolf lady at all? What if the person attacking the women was the ex that both Victoria and Michelle dated? What if he took their rings because he was jealous?

"What?" Antonio asked. "You have that look on your face."

"What look?"

"The one that says you just figured something out."

"I have a theory, that's all," I said. "I'll pass it along to the police."

"A motive?" Carmen asked, unable to keep to herself any longer.

"Maybe," I said. "And you might be right," I said to Antonio. "It might have been a guy after all. But he definitely wouldn't have been after me." Victoria and I may have had a man in common, but Michelle and I definitely didn't. Victoria had been the intended target after all.

I texted Jerry.

Maybe the two women were connected by a similar love interest.

Jerry texted back.

K

I rolled my eyes. That was it?

I wanted to respond with a lecture about how writing the letter K as the entire text message was impolite and frustrating. But I didn't think Jerry would give a damn.

This, however, changed my thoughts on going to the author signing in Big Mountain. If it was a man—a man they had both dated—it wouldn't be Becky Fredrickson. But I couldn't necessarily rule her out. Not until I talked to her, at least. She was the queen of the werewolves, after all.

Antonio, Sondra, and I closed the offices and banquet hall together. There were a few stragglers here and there, but no one even remotely threatening.

Shayla and Bella were back at their stroller-pushing

rollerblading, the lady with the dogs was busy training them to roll over in unison, and a few fishermen were soaking up the last bit of time in hopes of landing the big one.

"Why was that woman pushing a baby carriage with a fake baby?" Sondra said, interrupting the silence that had taken over the majority of our closing routine.

"Shayla?" I asked. "She's a police officer and used to be a summie."

"That's not what I asked," Sondra's tone made me want to stomp on her foot. "I asked why she would push a baby carriage with a fake baby."

Antonio let out a chuckle, and I wanted to stomp on his foot too.

"It's for balance with the rollerblades," I said. "And she's my best friend."

I walked away before Sondra could ask any more insulting questions. I'd laughed at Shayla's idea, but no one else was allowed to laugh at my best friend. Not while I was around anyway.

I hopped in my truck, backed out, and nearly ran over a woman standing in the middle of the road.

It was the woman with the dogs, though the dogs were nowhere in sight.

I rolled down my window. "Can I help you?"

She stepped up to the side of the truck. "Are you Rylie Cooper?"

I hated when park guests asked me that question. It meant they'd either seen me on YouTube or I'd given someone they knew a ticket.

"Yes," I said. "What can I do for you?"

She reached into her oversized purse and dug around for something. Who knew dog trainers were so weird?

"I saw you working with your dogs, they're amazing," I said. "My dog, Fizzy, is not great about doing tricks."

"They're working dogs," she murmured without looking up from her purse. "And maybe if you were more authoritative, he'd listen to you."

"Oh, he listens to me," I said, though that was a bit of a lie. Fizzy did whatever he wanted. But he didn't chew things up anymore, so that was a plus. "He's just a wild card."

"Dogs need a master," she said. "An alpha."

"Do you need a light?" I pulled my flashlight from my belt and shined it into her overly stuffed purse. I could see what looked like a book, several leashes, a poncho, a flashlight, and maybe some change reflecting at the bottom.

"Hold on." She swung her purse out of the beam of my flashlight. I guess if she wanted to use a flashlight, she would have used her own.

"Everything okay here?" Antonio and Sondra came walking up toward us.

It was that moment when the woman finally found what she was looking for. "Here." She handed me a notebook and a pen. "Can you sign this for me?"

YouTube it was.

"Do you want me to make it out to anyone?"

"Just sign your name."

I signed and handed it back to her.

"Thanks," she said. "My niece will be thrilled."

"No problem," I said as she shoved the notebook and

pen back into her purse, not minding the pages as they wrinkled. Maybe her niece didn't mean that much to her.

"The park is closing," Antonio said. "But you can come back tomorrow."

"I'm here every day," she said. "I train dogs. I'm sure you've seen me."

"Can't say that I have," Antonio said.

The woman deflated. Being brushed off by a hot guy was never fun.

"But I'll keep an eye out," he added.

She smiled, though she didn't look pleased. "Thanks, Rylie," she said before she turned and walked back up to her SUV, where I assumed the dogs had been contained, though they didn't bark at all when she opened the door.

Maybe she was right. Maybe I needed to be more authoritative with Fizzy. Or maybe she just had a stick up her ass. Fizzy was perfect just the way he was.

"I think she's the last one in the park," Antonio said, breaking me out of my thought spiral. "Let's lock up the gates."

The week went by in a flurry of rainy boringness. I worried that it would still be raining for my Saturday trip to the mountains, but it was a beautiful day for my favorite drive.

Too bad I had a babysitter.

Or should I say, several babysitters.

Shayla may or may not have *accidentally* let it slip that I was going up to the mountains to both Garrett *and* Jerry. Though, thankfully, she had left out the part about investigating when she told Garrett.

So here I was, driving Cherry Anne, top-down, my hair blowing in the breeze, with not only Garrett and Jerry but Shayla too. It was a packed car. Mustangs weren't exactly known for their big backseats.

The only benefit was that with the wind whipping all around us, it was nearly impossible to carry a conversation, which gave me plenty of time to think about how I would make all of this work.

Garrett was under the impression that we were

checking out the Big Mountain Lodge and Resort for our wedding venue, which was a possibility because the Big Mountain Lodge and Resort was the best venue in the entire state.

Jerry knew the truth. Shayla had weaseled it out of me that I was going to the author signing because I had a lead. And she didn't want me going alone. I tried to convince her she and I could go together, but that wasn't enough. She was still a rookie, and anything we came across could hurt her chances of becoming a full-fledged officer. Especially, if they knew she was investigating on her own . . . or with me.

Jerry hadn't asked any questions. He didn't know the details but apparently didn't much care about them anyway. Or maybe he'd get them out of me once Garrett wasn't around.

Either way, I wasn't thrilled about the arrangement.

When we dropped over the mountain pass and down into the heart of Big Mountain, my breath caught at the sight of the peaks surrounding the lake and the town I'd once called home. I didn't realize how much I missed it until now.

The temperature was almost always a solid ten or twenty degrees cooler than in Denver, and it felt amazing. Shayla pulled a jacket around her and Garrett kept incrementally turning up his side of the thermostat, but I couldn't bring myself to put the top up.

The sun shone down from a big blue sky, almost as if we were in a painting.

"It's beautiful up here." Garrett squeezed my thigh. "The perfect place for a wedding."

I thought I heard Jerry huff in the back seat, but it might have been my imagination.

When we pulled up to the Big Mountain Lodge and Resort, my stomach dropped. People were everywhere. We'd be lucky to find a parking spot, let alone get into the actual event.

"What's going on?" Garrett asked.

"Looks like some kind of event," Shayla said.

"Is this why Jerry came along?" Garrett whispered though I'm sure Jerry could hear him.

I shrugged. How could I tell him Jerry was there to help me investigate Victoria's attack and Michelle's murder?

"Pull up to that security guard," Jerry said, pointing for me to pull off the main driveway where we were lined up for parking. "I'm Jerry Delucci from the Prairie City Police Department. Can you please tell Meredith Dresden that I'm here to see her?"

The security officer's face paled. "Uh sure," he said, his voice cracking like a teenager's. He took a breath and pushed the button on his shoulder mic. "Chief, I have a Jerry Delucci here to see you."

"Park him in the back. I'll meet him there." The woman's voice was stern and authoritative.

"Right this way." The security officer led us to a private parking lot in the back.

Meredith Dresden—or rather, the Chief of the Big Mountain Police Department—met us at Cherry Anne and gave Jerry a big hug.

"Jerry, it's so good to see you," she said, then turned

her attention back to the security officer. "Get back to your post."

The security officer practically ran the other way.

"Still got your charm, I see," Jerry croaked.

"I don't recall you minding it when I was on your team."

Jerry laughed while we all watched the exchange. I'd never met Meredith, but Troy had talked about her a lot. She was his boss, after all.

"Who are your friends?" Meredith asked.

"I wouldn't exactly call them friends," Jerry said. "I just hitched a ride with them when I heard they were coming up to visit the place."

Meredith examined each of us.

"This is Shayla—one of the rookies I've told you about," Jerry said.

Shayla looked surprised that Jerry had spoken about her.

"Pleasure to meet you, Shayla," Meredith shook her hand.

"And this is Rylie Cooper—a park ranger in Prairie City —and her fiancé, Garrett," Jerry continued. "They wanted to check out the resort for their wedding."

"I'm sure Blake would love to show you around," Meredith said. "Let's go find her."

We followed Meredith in through the back of the main resort lodge, through a bunch of people dressed in costume, to an office with a spectacular view of the property.

"Blake, this is Garrett, Shayla, Rylie, and you know Jerry."

Blake, a woman I recognized from school—a few years ahead of me—sat behind an enormous desk with her long brown curls draped over her shoulders.

"It's nice to meet you." Blake shook all of our hands and gave Jerry a hug, making him turn the color of a tomato. "What can I do for you?"

"Garrett and Rylie are getting married," Jerry said. "They thought they'd check out the place."

We were getting in deep. Sure, I wanted to check out the place, but I'd been here hundreds of times. What I needed was to get to that author's event.

"Normally, I'd be happy to show you around," Blake said. "But as you could see, we're busy today with the event."

Garrett squeezed my hand as if to tell me it would be okay.

"But I can get one of my assistants to give you the tour."

"That would be great," Garrett said, his voice excited.

"While you do that," Jerry said. "Meredith and I are going to catch up."

"Why doesn't Shayla come with us?" Meredith said. "I'd love to hear about her time as a rookie in the big city."

Shayla nodded with a grin on her face.

Great. Shayla was supposed to help cover for me with Garrett so I could talk to some people and hopefully find Becky Frederickson.

She shrugged an apology back at me as she followed Jerry and Meredith out the door.

"This is my assistant, Zen." Blake introduced us to a

man who looked like he was barely out of high school. "He'll give you the tour and answer any wedding questions you may have."

We both thanked her and followed Zen out of the office.

"Let's start with the date." Zen pulled out his smartphone calendar. "When would you like to book your wedding?"

"If we go with you," I said.

Zen smirked. "I guess it's always an if until it's a yes."

"December seventh."

"You're in luck," Zen said. "We've just had a cancellation. December seventh is open. Let me check one more thing." He scrolled through his phone. "Yes, as I thought, there is no waiting list for that date. Would you like me to pencil you in?"

"Do we have to put down a deposit?" Garrett asked.

I knew my parents would be fine with whatever venue —especially the Big Mountain Lodge and Resort—but I didn't know how putting down deposits worked when they were paying for the wedding. "Don't you think I should talk to my parents first?"

"I can put down the deposit if needed," Garrett said.

"I'll pencil you in." Zen tapped furiously on his phone. "But I will need a deposit by the end of the weekend to make it certain. I'll tell you one thing, if you don't snatch up this date, it'll be gone before Monday afternoon."

I hated it when people pressured me into things. But he had a point.

"Why don't you show us around so we can make an informed decision," Garrett said.

The last thing I wanted to do was walk around the resort, but Garrett seemed so excited, so I put on my happy face.

"Have you ever been to Big Mountain before?" Zen walked us past the ballroom where the book signing was taking place. I tried to sneak a peek, but Garrett squeezed my hand, bringing me back to the conversation.

"Uh, yeah," I said. "I grew up here."

"Did you know Blake?" Zen's eyes widened.

"She was a few years ahead of me, but I knew of her."

"You're fortunate to have grown up in such a beautiful place," Zen said. "I assume you've been to the resort then?"

"Many times." I nodded. "We used to swim in the pool on weekends."

"I'm surprised you didn't think of it for the wedding before now," Garrett said.

"My brain must have been stuck on ski resorts."

"Ah yes, a wedding on top of a mountain can be lovely," Zen said.

"But I don't know how to ski or snowboard, so this would probably be a better option," Garrett said.

I sighed and glanced back toward the event, catching the slightest glimpse of a purple robe walking into the ballroom.

"I need to use the restroom," I said. "I'll catch up with—"

"Rylie?"

The voice stopped me in my tracks.

No.

Not here.

Not now.

"Rylie, is that you?"

When I turned back, Troy and a tiny blonde woman stood staring at me while Garrett looked between the two of us in consternation.

"Officer, is something wrong?" Zen asked.

"Zen, you've known me since the day you started working here." Troy patted Zen's head affectionately, making Zen blush. "You can call me Troy."

"Troy," Garrett said.

"And you are?" Troy asked.

"This is Garrett." I stepped in. "My fiancé."

Troy's face paled, but he recovered quickly and reached out to shake Garrett's hand. "It's nice to meet the guy who finally got Rylie to settle down."

"What do you mean, settle down?" I asked. "It wasn't me who had a problem committing."

"The pleasure is all mine," Garrett said, stopping me from continuing.

Troy wasn't in uniform but light jeans and a short-sleeved button-down shirt. He wasn't short by any stretch of the imagination, but compared to Garrett, he looked small.

"What are you doing here?" Troy asked, not trying in the slightest to be polite. "I thought you left Big Mountain forever."

The woman next to him shifted from one foot to the other, obviously uncomfortable.

"I never said that," I said. "Big Mountain is my home, and it's where we're getting married." I tucked myself under Garrett's arm, and he squeezed my shoulder. "Zen here has our wedding scheduled and everything."

"That's great," Troy said. "Maybe I'll get married here someday too."

The blonde's eyes widened with a deer in the headlights look.

"Why aren't you with Victoria?" I asked. "She's still in the hospital, you know."

If he was cheating on his fiancée while she was on her deathbed, I might punch him right in the middle of the corridor.

"I know she's still in the hospital," he said, but then his phone rang. "I have to take this." Troy looked at Garrett. "Good luck with her, dude." He put the phone to his ear and began walking down the hall, the blonde following silently after him.

If I were in a cartoon, steam would have rushed out my ears and nose.

Zen, Garrett, and I stood in silence for a moment. Then Zen cleared his throat. "Does that mean you'd like to put down the deposit?"

"Absolutely," I said.

"Why don't you take that bathroom break." Garrett squeezed me one more time. "And I'll get everything figured out with the deposit."

I looked up at him, and some of my anger melted away, replaced by excitement. I was going to marry this massively handsome man at the resort of my dreams—a man who would never cheat on me whether I was conscious or not.

"Thanks, babe," I said.

Garrett bent down and kissed me so tenderly it made me want to grab his head and smash his lips up against mine. But I resisted.

"I'll catch up with you when I'm done," I said. However, I had no intention of catching back up with them.

I had a wolf-lady in a purple cape to interview.

18

I bypassed the bathroom and went directly to the ballroom, where I was utterly overwhelmed by the sheer number of people in costume. But even with very little room to move, it wasn't hard to find Becky.

If the author was the number one celebrity in the room, Becky seemed like a close second.

I pushed my way through the crowd and got within earshot of the queen of the wolves.

"Becky Frederickson?" I shouted over the endless chatter of fangirls surrounding her.

The surrounding crowd hushed.

"I'm sorry, I don't know a Becky Frederickson." She winked. "I'm Bantasma, queen of the werewolves."

I did my best not to snicker. "Yes, uh, sorry," I said. "Bantasma. May I have a moment of your time?"

"Get in line." Another woman dressed as a werewolf pointed across the room where I assumed the line ended.

"This is official business." I inched closer. "I need to speak with you about possible theft and murder charges."

Her admirers gasped.

"Murder charges?" Becky gaped at me. "I don't know what you're talking about."

But she very quickly stepped away—much to the disappointment of her onlookers—and followed me into the hall.

"Why would you say such horrible things in front of my friends?" Becky asked. "What happened to that woman was downright ghastly."

"What happened to both women was ghastly." I wasn't giving in to her sweet and innocent routine. "So why'd you do it?"

"Two women?" She brushed pieces of her hair behind her ears and adjusted her crown.

"That's some nice jewelry you have there." I decided on a different approach. I pointed to the various rings on her hands. "Did you steal those from your victims?"

"You can't seriously think I had anything to do with this." Her eyes were glazing over with tears.

"Why not?" I crossed my arms over my chest. "From where I stand, you seem to be a likely suspect."

"Because of my costume jewelry?" A tear trickled down her cheek. She pulled off the rings. "Here, look."

I was no expert on rings, but these were obviously plastic. I handed them back.

"Plus, when that woman was attacked, I was surrounded by at least twenty people."

"Your admirers?" I asked. "I'm sure they'd never turn you in. Heck, they may have even helped."

"I never even met that woman."

Now I had her.

I pulled out my phone and showed her the screen. "You never met her, huh?"

She took the phone from my hand and studied the photo. "This is the woman who died?"

I didn't reply.

She looked up at me, something like fear etched across her face.

"It looks like the two of you were arguing."

She handed me back my phone. "She was upset that we were blocking the trail. I think she was doing a timed run or something. She just kept screaming at us."

"Did that make you mad?"

"Well, it didn't make me happy," Becky said. "But I would have never hurt her. Honestly, if my club members hadn't been close, she might have tried to hurt me."

It was hard to think negatively of someone who had died a horrible death. But everyone had their flaws. Could she have taken her frustrations out on the wrong person and gotten herself into trouble?

"Look, if you need someone to corroborate my story, I'll take you to the person who hates me most in this entire world."

"Who is that?"

"Helgase, the vampire leader."

This was getting weird.

"And you were with this Helgase when?"

"Helgase follows me around at these events." She looked around and pointed to a woman dressed in head-to-toe vampire garb down the hallway. "See? She is always watching me."

"Why's that?"

"Because the vampires are the protectors in the story."

"And the werewolves are?"

"We're the misunderstood evil forces." She giggled in the least evil way possible. "Helgase just takes it way too seriously. And if anyone stole jewelry, it would be her."

Helgase looked like she was wearing just about every piece of jewelry in the known world.

"Let's go chat with her." But before we could make it five steps down the hallway, we heard a scream coming from the bathroom.

I left Bantasma in the hall and ran toward the scream.

I pushed through the bathroom door to find a woman looking into the wheelchair-accessible stall with her hand clapped over her mouth.

When I reached her side, it was apparent why she was so upset.

A tiny woman lay in a pile on the floor, beaten to a pulp just like Michelle and Victoria—sunglasses and all.

Behind me, a group of people entered, including three men—my ex, my fiancé, and a man who crumpled to the floor when he saw the woman.

I rushed to the woman's side and felt for a pulse, but I felt nothing. I started CPR. "You." I pointed to a woman who seemed the least worked up. "Call 9-1-1."

"Oh my God." Troy peered into the stall. "Olivia?"

The pieces clicked together. This woman had been the one with Troy only minutes before.

"You don't get to say her name, you smoldering pile of dog shit," the man on the floor yelled up at Troy.

Troy's face was white as a ghost.

The man on the floor grabbed Olivia's hand. "Her ring," he said. "It's gone." He turned his attention to Troy. "You did this." He stood and jabbed a finger right in the middle of Troy's chest. "You were mad she didn't want you anymore. She loves me. You had your chance."

Troy looked like he might be sick. He didn't say anything.

Mark—one of my old firefighter buddies—walked in. "Okay, that's enough." He put his massive frame between the two men. "Troy, why don't you wait outside."

Mark glanced in my direction. "Hey, Rylie. Long time."

He took over compressions, and another firefighter started hooking up the AED.

"Please tell me you're not here for him." Mark motioned toward Troy.

"Nope," I said. "My fiancé's right there." I pointed toward Garrett, who gave a small wave.

"Bring him by the station before you leave," Mark said. "I'm sure the guys would love to meet him."

I stood and walked past all the people right into Garrett's arms.

"Are you okay?" he asked.

"I'm fine," I said, letting him embrace me.

I wasn't fine. I was anything but fine. This was the second woman tied to Troy who had been attacked. Maybe even the third. And if that was the case, I could be next.

Becky peeked in the door.

"Can you excuse me for just a minute?" I asked Garrett.

He looked confused but nodded.

"I guess I owe you an apology," I said to Becky.

She nodded. "This makes number three, right?"

"Yep," I said.

"I hope you find who's doing this."

"Me too."

I glanced down the hall. Troy was nowhere in sight.

19

"What's going on?" Meredith pushed her way through the crowd, closely followed by Jerry and Shayla.

"Her name is Olivia," I said. "She was attacked in what looks like the same manner as the two women at Alder Ridge Reservoir."

"How so?" Meredith asked.

"Her ring is missing, the marks on her body look like a similar object caused them, and the attacker left the signature pair of aviator sunglasses on her face."

Meredith raised an eyebrow. "Good observations. Anything else?"

"Her fiancé is the man holding her hand. He accused Troy of doing this. Apparently, she and Troy were together at some point," I said. "I also saw them together earlier today."

"I'm impressed. What did you say your name was?"

"Rylie Cooper."

"Any chance you'd be interested in joining your hometown police department?"

There were so many reasons why that would be a terrible idea, but I was flattered nonetheless. "Not at this point." It never hurt to keep my options open. "But thank you."

"Where did Troy go?" she asked.

"He walked outside when the firefighters got here."

Meredith nodded. "Thanks for your help."

I nearly jumped three feet when I felt a hand at the small of my back.

"Just me," Garrett said. "Why don't we get out of here?"

He led us out of the bathroom, Shayla and Jerry following along behind.

"I think I'll see if Meredith needs any help," Jerry said. "Don't leave without me."

Once we were in the lodge's lobby, Garrett squeezed my hand. "I have to tell you I'm really impressed."

"You're impressed?" I asked. "With what?"

Shayla smiled.

"As much as I hate to say it, you seem to be very good at investigation work. Your observations were remarkable. I would never have noticed those things."

"She may get herself into some tight spots, but you're right, she has an eye—and a talent—for investigation," Shayla said.

"When you were telling Meredith about the case, you lit up," Garrett said. "Your entire face glowed."

"You guys are sweet, but it's not a big deal," I said.

"But maybe it is," Garrett said, not letting me off the

hook so quickly. "Maybe I was too hard on you when I said I didn't want you investigating."

"Really?" I couldn't believe he was saying those words. Maybe the altitude was getting to him.

"I know I worry too much, but I'll butt out. I'm sorry."

He kissed me and gave me a big hug, and I had to wipe tears out of the corners of my eyes.

"Now, should we look around some more? Since I've got us all set up to get married here in December?"

Shayla squealed. "Really?"

"Yep," I said. "I couldn't resist. It's just so beautiful."

"We have to choose between the barn, the event center, and the field," Garrett started rattling off all the information Zen had given him. "I think the field might be cold for a winter wedding, but I'm open to it if that's what you want."

"What do you want?" I asked.

"I think my preference would be the event center. But let's look at it before we decide."

He led Shayla and me back through the lodge and out to the various venues. The entire time he talked about the pros and cons of every area.

Not once did I see Meredith or Troy, and by the time we were finished walking what felt like the entire grounds, I was exhausted and had no interest in taking Garrett to the fire station. I shot Mark a quick text and told him we wouldn't make it this time.

Jerry was waiting for us at Cherry Anne, his foot tapping out an impatient code.

"What took you so long?" he asked. "I've been waiting forever."

"You could have texted us," Shayla said.

"Or you could have been on time." Jerry huffed.

"Sorry," Garrett said. "That was my fault. I got so excited about all the wedding plans. I lost track of time."

When we got in the car, Jerry said, "You impressed Meredith today."

What was it with all these people being impressed by my noticing sunglasses and a missing ring?

"She wasn't the only one," Shayla said. "Garrett was too."

"Truth." Garrett rubbed a hand over my kneecap as I sped up the mountain. I had the top up since it was past dark, and the temperatures would be frigid the higher I climbed up the pass.

"I guess investigating crimes isn't such a terrible thing after all," I said with a smirk.

"As long as you're careful," Garrett said. "And you won't get fired."

"My job's pretty secure at this point," I said.

"Just watch out for Detective Bryant," Jerry croaked out. "He doesn't seem to like you much."

"The feeling's mutual," I said. "Did Meredith find Troy?"

"Why would Meredith be looking for Troy?" Shayla must not have heard my conversation with Meredith in the bathroom.

"Because he's now a suspect in the case," Jerry said. "And no, she didn't find him. He vanished."

"Wait, they think your ex-boyfriend might have had something to do with these attacks?" Garrett asked. "But why?"

I shrugged and looked back at Jerry.

"Motive's unclear," he said. "But we know he is connected to at least two of the women."

"One is his current fiancée," I said. "And the other seemed to be an ex—at least by what her fiancé was saying."

"It doesn't make much sense," Shayla said.

"None at all," I said. "I just don't think Troy could do something like this. He may have been a cheater, but he wasn't violent."

"But then why did he disappear?" Garrett asked.

"Maybe he didn't," I said. "Maybe he just went home or back to see Victoria."

"That woman looked awfully uncomfortable with him when we saw them," Garrett said.

"You saw them together?" Shayla asked.

I nodded. "Only a few minutes before the attack. But they were walking away from the bathrooms."

"Speaking of bathrooms," Garrett said. "You were in the bathroom. Did you see anything happen?"

My stomach clenched. "I was on my way to the bathroom when I saw someone I wanted to talk to. Next thing I knew, there was screaming."

I saw Jerry and Shayla exchange looks in my rearview mirror.

"I guess it's good you weren't there. if Troy is attacking ex-girlfriends and stealing their engagement rings . . ."

I looked at my ring. I probably shouldn't be wearing it, but I'd only recently gotten used to it being on my finger. "I really don't think it was Troy."

Garrett looked away.

"Not that I'm defending him," I said. "I mean, I guess it could have been him. Maybe when we get back, Victoria will wake up, and she can tell us everything."

But I knew she hadn't woken up because every text I'd gotten from Ursula that day was asking for updates on the case. If Victoria were awake, Ursula wouldn't need updates. Someone would be behind bars.

20

"There's a guard at the hospital watching Victoria's room, right?" I asked Shayla the next morning after not being able to sleep all night. The sleepless nights were going to catch up with me soon if I wasn't careful.

"There should be." She handed me a plate of over-easy eggs and wheat toast.

"Thanks," I said. "I was just thinking, if Victoria wakes up, she could tell us who attacked her, and the attacker wouldn't want that, right?"

"Right," Shayla said. "Which is why I'm sure they have someone watching out for her."

I couldn't chance it. I had to make sure for myself.

But first, I wanted to talk to Michelle's fiancé.

Ursula had given me his information days ago, but I hadn't known what to say. Now, I needed to know if Troy and Michelle had ever been involved.

"Hi, Frederick?" I asked when who I assumed to be Michelle's fiancé opened the door of a small farmhouse about twenty minutes outside of town.

"Freddy," he said. "Who's asking."

"Rylie Cooper," I said. "I'm a park ranger at the Alder Ridge Reservoir. I'm so sorry for your loss."

The man only came up to my chin. He and Michelle must have made quite the odd couple. And if he was her type, Troy definitely wasn't.

"I've already spoken to the police. I have nothing else to say." He started to close the door.

"Did Michelle ever date someone named Troy Shipley?"

"Doesn't ring a bell." He didn't open the door back up but didn't close it any further either. "Michelle and I were together for the better part of three years. Before that, she didn't date much."

I pulled out my phone and showed him Troy's picture on a social media profile I no longer followed. "This is Troy," I said. "Does he look familiar?"

He shook his head. "But that woman does." He pointed at the woman standing next to Troy.

I looked more closely. The woman wasn't Victoria.

"She does?" I asked.

"I think I saw her jogging down our street a couple of times," he said. "And since we live so far out of town, we don't get many joggers."

"Can you tell me anything else about her?" I glanced back at the photo. It was a miracle he recognized her at all. The picture was completely pixilated, and her blonde hair partially covered her face.

"I don't know," he said. "Maybe it wasn't her. But I know I've never seen him."

"Thanks," I said. "And again, I'm so sorry for your loss."

"Michelle was amazing. I was lucky to find her." He sniffed. "I hope you find out who did this."

"Me too."

My mind had the information on a loop. Victoria and Olivia dated Troy. The woman in the picture with Troy—not Victoria—had possibly been scoping out Michelle's house.

I pulled my phone out as I drove back down the road toward town. Troy's profile picture had changed. Now it was just a sunset.

Damnit. I should have taken a screenshot of the photo while it was still up.

I searched futilely through the rest of his profile, but it was locked down tighter than the maximum-security prison he'd end up in if they found him guilty of attacking these women.

And what about the woman in the picture not being Victoria? Did that mean he wasn't engaged to Victoria?

If he wasn't, that made his involvement in the attacks more likely. Especially if he was having issues with his exes getting engaged.

I nearly drove off the road when a car honked because I was drifting into their lane. I dropped the phone on the seat and took a couple of deep breaths.

Troy knew I was engaged too. He'd seen the ring. If he was responsible for the attacks, I could be next.

His reaction to finding out I was engaged flashed in my mind. That weird look on his face.

I pulled the ring off my finger and locked it inside the glove box for safekeeping. Not that I'd care that my ring got stolen if I was dead.

Victoria was still unconscious when I arrived at the hospital. A man who was most definitely not Troy sat next to her holding her hand.

"I take it you're Victoria's fiancé?" I asked.

"I am," he said. "I'm sorry, I don't think we've met?"

"I'm Rylie Cooper. I worked with—"

"Victoria talked about you a lot." He didn't stand to shake my hand. He looked exhausted. "It's nice to meet you."

"Same here," I said. "I wish it was under different circumstances. How is she doing?"

"Not great," he said. "They don't know if she'll come out of the coma."

"I didn't see a guard outside," I said. "Shouldn't someone be watching her room?"

"I guess they're leaving that up to me," he said. "I'm an agent."

"FBI?"

He nodded. "No one will hurt her when I'm around."

"That's good." I didn't know what else to say. I'd gotten what I came to find out. She wasn't engaged to Troy, and she had protection.

"Ursula said you're looking into the case?"

"You'd probably do a better job." Why hadn't Ursula asked her FBI fiancé to look into it instead?

"Too close to the situation," he said. "Plus, Ursula doesn't trust me."

"Why not?"

"I didn't protect her niece like I promised when I asked for her hand in marriage."

"You asked her aunt for her hand?"

"Her aunt and her mom," he said. "They became something of a parenting duo after her dad—Ursula's brother—died when Victoria was eleven."

"Victoria was pretty excited about the engagement," I said. "She couldn't wait to show off her ring."

He rubbed her finger where the ring would have been. "It's too bad whoever did this took it."

"They have a thing for engagement rings."

"So I hear."

He probably knew more about the case than I did.

"What else do you know?" he asked.

"Three women, all engaged, all the rings gone."

He nodded, not looking away from Victoria's face.

"Suspects include a wolf lady—Becky Frederickson—though, I don't think she did it. There's also the ex-boyfriend and—"

"The millionaire stoner?"

I'd forgotten about Ansel.

"Ansel isn't responsible," I said. "I was with him when Victoria was attacked, and I don't think he was even at the event over the weekend."

"But you were," he said, finally looking at me.

"I was," I said slowly.

"And you were there when Victoria was attacked *and* when the first woman was attacked."

"Yes." I knew where he was going with this.

He stood, giving Victoria's hand one last squeeze.

"I also know about your history with Victoria."

He stalked toward me, almost like a predator. I held my ground. I had nothing to hide, but I also didn't want to give anything away. "What do you mean?"

"Don't play dumb. I know she cheated on me. With your boyfriend. The same one who cheated on you with Michelle and Olivia. Those are their names, right?"

I swallowed. How did he know all of this?

"FBI, remember?" he said as if answering my silent question.

"Those weren't the only three he cheated on you with, you know?"

I didn't want to hear this. I came to make sure Victoria was protected. And now I was being attacked.

"How many more will you attack—kill?"

"I didn't attack or kill anyone."

"I bet you have Victoria's DNA on your baton."

I thought about it and, of course, I did. I'd set it next to her—in her blood. Plus, she'd pinched her finger in it when she was playing with it in the truck.

"I heard the recording from the radio that night. It sounded a lot like she was begging you for mercy."

"She was calling me for help." I couldn't stand here and let him accuse me of this. I turned to leave the room.

"Where's your ring?"

I whipped back around. "I took it off."

"Did your guy get smart and dump you when he found out you were still hung up on your ex?"

"I took it off because it seems like someone is targeting Troy's exes, and I don't want to be the next victim."

"How can you be the victim when you're the attacker?"

I was about to leave when a blood-curdling scream came from the bed.

Victoria was awake and screaming at the top of her lungs.

Her fiancé—whose name I'd never gotten—rushed over to her.

"Rylie, no!" Victoria screamed.

"I'm here," I said.

"Please stop," Victoria said as her fiancé tried to calm her. "Rylie!"

A nurse rushed in and tried to help calm Victoria down.

"Who did this?" her fiancé asked. "Did Rylie attack you?"

Victoria answered by letting out another scream that would make dogs bark and glass shatter, then passed out.

"Vic?" Her fiancé was shaking her. "Victoria, wake up."

But she had gone back to her comatose state.

The nurse checked her vitals.

"Is she okay?" I asked.

"Get out," her fiancé yelled. "Get the hell out of here."

I hesitated for only a second before I turned and walked out.

As the door closed behind me, I heard him say, "Don't leave town, the police will want to speak with you."

21

I called Shayla in tears when I got to my car.

"Slow down," Shayla said. "What happened?"

"Victoria's fiancé thinks I attacked her and the other women."

"Her fiancé? As in Troy?"

"No, she's not engaged to Troy. She's engaged to some bigshot FBI agent who thinks I am trying to kill all the women Troy cheated on me with."

"He cheated on you with all of them?"

"And more, I guess." Even though I was over him, it still sucked to know how unimportant our relationship was to him. "And if there were others, they're probably in danger."

"Just like you are," she said. "I know you said before you didn't think it could be Troy, but . . ."

"It was unlikely when I thought he was engaged to Victoria, but if he's mad that his exes are getting engaged, it would make more sense." I looked at the glove box. "He did give me a strange look when he found out I was engaged. At least I think he did. It might have also been because I barfed on him. It's hard to know."

"I talked to Meredith today," she said. "Troy is gone. No one has seen him since Olivia was attacked."

"I have a bad feeling about this," I said. "I think I'll leave the rest of the investigation to the police. Especially since they're probably on their way to arrest me."

"The FBI might be, but I've heard nothing about you being a suspect. It's absurd."

"I'll call Ursula and let her know I'm bowing out."

"Okay," Shayla said. "I'll see you at home tonight. And Rylie?"

"Yeah?"

"Be careful."

"If anything happens to me, my ring is in my glove compartment. Make sure Garrett gets it back."

"Nothing will happen to you."

We disconnected, and I called Ursula.

"I can't do this anymore," I said. "Your future nephew-in-law thinks I'm responsible for hurting Victoria and killing Michelle and I don't even know if Olivia is alive or dead or—"

"Rylie, stop."

I stopped.

"Take a breath."

I did.

"Elliot is an idiot," she said. "He may work for the FBI, but he has no idea what he's talking about. He's just mad that someone hurt the woman he loves most in the world."

"He may be an idiot, but I'm done. If this guy is going after my ex-boyfriend's flings, I could be next."

"Your ex-boyfriend's flings?"

"Victoria sort of dated the guy I was dating." I held my breath waiting for her reply.

"Why didn't you tell me this sooner?"

"I figured if Victoria didn't want to say anything, I didn't need to either."

"So Victoria knew you before she took the job?"

"From what I can tell, yes."

"Who dated him first?"

"I did," I said, not wanting to throw Victoria's name through the wood chipper of infidelity.

"So she dated him before Elliot, and you dated him before her?"

"Sort of."

"Rylie, just tell me."

"Victoria slept with my boyfriend. I caught them in bed together. Elliot knows, and I guess he forgave her."

"That *would* make you look suspicious," Ursula said.

"Especially since he cheated on me with a lot of women. Including the other two who were attacked."

"And you were there when they were all attacked."

"Yes," I said. "And stoner-Ansel was the only one with me when Victoria was attacked. He lost his memory so he can't attest to that. But, I swear, I didn't do it."

"How in the world did you work with Victoria when you knew she slept with your boyfriend?"

"I didn't want to lose my job. The only route was to be professional."

Ursula was silent on the other end of the line.

"So I just wanted you to know I'm not investigating anymore. In fact, I might be in jail and unable to work too."

Ursula sighed. "You were with Nikki just moments before Michelle was attacked. She can attest to that."

She was right. I had a better alibi than I thought. "And when Victoria was being attacked, I went into the office that she had already locked and armed. I was the only one in the park other than Victoria, who had a key."

"So, you couldn't have been attacking Victoria and in the office at the same time."

"Exactly." I sighed a breath of relief. Maybe Elliot was being accusatory because he was grieving.

"Does that mean you'll still look into the case?" Ursula's voice was the nicest I'd ever heard it.

"I'll think about it."

I knew something was wrong before I even got to my door. My duty belt with my only two forms of protection hung on a hook next to the door. The door that was ajar.

Shayla wasn't supposed to be home for another few hours.

Someone was inside.

I shot off a quick text to Garrett.

Are you at my apartment?

He replied quickly.

No. Everything okay?

Not sure. If I don't call in five minutes, call the police.

I shoved my phone back in my pocket and took a

breath. If I wasn't worried about Fizzy, I would have gone back to my car and called the police myself.

I could only hope he'd run away and wasn't inside hurt.

I peeked through the crack of the door but saw nothing amiss. It didn't look like anyone had stolen anything.

The door opened silently thanks to the Crisco spray Shayla used on the hinges a week or so ago.

I pulled my baton and pepper spray from my belt, extending the baton as quietly as I could, which wasn't quietly enough.

Fizzy's roar came from the bathroom. His bark would scare just about anyone, let alone his sharp teeth.

Whoever was inside had been able to get Fizzy into the bathroom. The room he hated the most in the world. For some reason, he was terrified of the toilet.

But from the sound of his barks and clawing at the door, he'd gotten over his fear and was out for blood.

"Shut up, butt licker," a man's voice shouted from my bedroom.

If I could only open that bathroom door, I wouldn't need to use my baton. Fizzy might not walk in a line or do magic tricks, but I was one hundred percent certain he would protect me against a bear if he needed to.

I tip-toed down the hallway, my fingers—grasping the pepper spray—inches from the bathroom door handle when a drawer slammed.

He was looking for something.

I tried to twist the handle, but nothing. It was locked.

Smart.

I backed my way down the hallway toward the front door.

Fizzy was okay for the moment. I needed to call the police.

But the man exited my room, and we locked eyes.

The man was Troy. I should have known when he called Fizzy butt licker.

I raised my baton with my right hand. Just like I had in training.

The question was, could I use it on him?

The pepper spray was in my other hand, but like Victoria, pepper spray didn't affect Troy. He'd bragged about it for months after his training.

"Whoa, Rylie, put that thing down."

"What are you doing here?"

"I wanted to see you. We need to talk."

"You locked my dog in the bathroom and went through my stuff. You could have just called."

He laughed a little. "Where's your ring?"

"Why do you care?" I asked. "Are you starting a collection?"

"I was going to ask you the same thing."

"I didn't hurt those women. I had no idea you cheated on me with the other two, or however many others there were."

He didn't even look ashamed to be outed. "A guy has needs."

"How does your current girlfriend feel about that?"

"Hilary?" His eyes shifted. "How do you know about Hilary?"

"I saw her in your profile picture."

"Stalker much?"

"Shut up, Troy," I said. "I was showing Michelle's fiancé your picture."

"Michelle's fiancé doesn't know me."

"No," I said. "But he recognized Hilary. Why'd you take the profile picture down?"

"People don't need to be in my business."

He was walking toward me now.

I gripped the baton more tightly. "Why would Hilary be stalking one of your ex-girlfriends?"

"Michelle was not a girlfriend." He laughed.

"Oh, just a fling?"

"At least you had the title."

"Yes, please tell me how lucky I was to be called your girlfriend." I rolled my eyes. "Maybe Hilary doesn't appreciate your cheating ass. Maybe she's attacking your ex-lovers."

"If she were smart, she'd attack my current lovers."

My earlier thought went out the window. I'd definitely be able to hit Troy. He was the biggest ass in the world.

He took another step toward me.

"Stay back," I said. "Or better yet, come at me and give me a reason to give you what you deserve."

My heart raced.

"You'd never hit me."

"I wouldn't test that theory."

Behind me, someone yelled, "Police."

My attention shifted just enough for Troy to charge me. But he didn't tackle me, he rammed his head into my baton and then fell to the ground screaming, "Help me!"

"Drop your weapons," the officer behind me said. I

dropped the baton right on top of Troy and almost laughed out loud when it hit him right in his nuts.

"The pepper spray too."

I dropped it.

Within seconds, my hands were cuffed behind my back, and I was being read my rights.

"I did nothing wrong," I said. "He broke into my apartment and locked up my dog. He was going through my bedroom."

"She's lying." He stood. A large red line crossed his face and forehead. A line that looked identical to the ones on the three women. They would easily think I was the attacker.

I didn't recognize any of the officers.

They didn't have on Prairie City Police Department uniforms on.

They were FBI.

They took me to Luke's station. Detective Bryant's station. Shayla and Jerry's station.

They booked me like a common criminal.

No matter how much I told them Troy was the attacker—the murderer—they acted like they couldn't hear me.

Within hours I was in a concrete cell.

The jailer walked by a couple of times before starting a conversation.

"What are you in for?"

I looked up at the tiny window in the door. I could only see her eyes and a small bit of her hair, but she seemed familiar. "Nothing. I did absolutely nothing wrong."

She laughed. "Everyone does something wrong."

"If I did something wrong, it was staying with the same dirtbag for five years. But that's not a crime."

"Attacking his exes is though," she said.

"Why'd you ask if you already knew?" I had no patience for her games.

"Wanted to hear it from you."

"I'll say it again. I did nothing illegal. I would never hurt anyone."

"Officer Shipley's face would say differently."

"Officer Shipley is an asshole."

She raised her eyebrows.

"But he ran into my baton. I didn't hit him with it."

"I should use that the next time I get taken in for an excessive force review."

For some reason—maybe it was the way she said those words—it clicked. She was the woman from the reservoir with the perfectly trained dogs.

"How's your niece?" I asked.

She hesitated as if she didn't expect me to recognize her. "Uh—my—uh—she's fine."

"Did she like the autograph?"

"Yep. Hung it in her room."

"You know, Officer Shipley locked my dog in the bathroom—the place my dog is most afraid of in the entire world."

She turned away from the window so I couldn't see her reaction.

Then I heard a key go into the door, and the heavy metal door slid open.

Detective Bryant stood on the other side. "Rylie, I can't say it's good to see you."

"Same here."

"Let's go have a chat."

I'd sat across from Detective Bryant in this room one too

many times. But this time, it was different. We weren't allies. And he wouldn't go easy on me.

"I've convinced the FBI to let me interrogate you since we have something of a history."

I nodded.

"Tell me what happened today at your apartment."

I went through the story in as much relevant detail as possible. I wasn't giving up anything else, though. If he wanted to know what I knew, he'd have to ask. I was done telling people what I thought happened just to have them shut me out.

"Officer Shipley tells a different story," Bryant said.

"That's no surprise," I said. "He's the best liar I've ever known."

"He said you asked him to come over so you could talk about what happened between the two of you."

"I'm engaged," I said. "There's nothing we need to talk about."

Bryant looked through his notes. "There's nothing in my notes about an engagement ring. Officer Shipley said you and your fiancé recently separated."

"Why don't you ask my fiancé if that's the case. Because it's not. My ring is locked in Cherry Anne's glove compartment."

"Why would you lock your ring in the glove compartment of your car?"

"Because I didn't want it to be the reason someone tried to kill me."

"You think someone would kill you for your ring?"

"That's what they took from the other women, maybe

that was the motive." It wasn't, not the ring itself anyway. Maybe what it represented.

Bryant gave me a tiny smile. "Do you think that was the motive?"

"Sure." I shrugged and leaned back in my chair. "Why not? Victoria's ring was probably worth a lot of money. I'm guessing that sleazeball Elliot paid a pretty penny to prove his love to his cheating girlfriend."

I could only hope Elliot was behind the one-way glass listening to this conversation.

"It sounds like you have a lot of animosity toward Victoria. That is who you're talking about, right? The woman you caught in bed with Officer Shipley? The reason the two of you broke up."

"Not really," I said. "She did me a favor." If only Troy were behind the glass too.

Bryant nodded. "Tell me about the other two women. Had you ever met them before?"

"Nope. I didn't even know they existed. But the FBI knows all about Officer Shipley's extra-curricular lovers."

I could picture Troy and Elliot standing next to each other behind the glass. Troy shrinking, knowing the man he stood next to knew of all the women he'd slept with.

"Why are you smiling?" Bryant asked.

"No reason." I looked past him at the glass.

He turned and looked too before returning his gaze to me. "Is there someone you'd like to speak with instead of me?"

"Oh sure," I said. "Lots of people. Starting with an attorney." I was done with this charade. He and I both knew I wasn't responsible for this.

"You're absolutely entitled to an attorney. You do not have to answer any of my questions."

I crossed my arms over my chest.

"But you may have something to say about this."

He opened his file and pulled out two photographs.

"These are pictures of the dresser drawers in your bedroom."

I leaned forward to look. They certainly seemed to be. They included my haphazardly thrown collection of thongs, bras, and socks.

But they also included items that made my heart stop beating.

Three rings and several pairs of aviator sunglasses.

24

"What can you tell me about those?"

"I don't know how they got there." I stopped and thought. "Actually, I have a good idea. Troy put them there when he broke into my apartment and locked up my dog."

"Your official statement is that you're being framed for the murder of two women and the attack on one other?"

"Did Victoria die?" Panic welled up inside me.

"Olivia did."

Tears stung at my eyes. It was hard to be thankful one woman was alive when another wasn't. "I'd like to speak to my attorney now."

Bryant took the photos and tucked them back into his file, just like the investigators did on TV.

I was in deep shit. It was my word against Troy's, and Troy was a cop. A lying sack of horse crap cop, but he was a cop.

"Come on, back to your cell," Miss Alpha herself pulled me up from my seat and led me back down the hall. "Looks like you might be here for a while. Too bad you had just as hard of a time training your man as you did your dog."

Her tone of voice made me want to punch her in the throat. But that would only give her—them—ammunition against me. Plus, my arms were restrained.

I tried to fall asleep on the rock-hard cardboard-thin mattress, but even with exhaustion practically seeping from my pores, I couldn't doze off.

Miss Alpha had gotten off shift hours ago, and the one who replaced her barely even walked down the hall.

I knew how things went. Tomorrow morning my attorney would talk to me, we'd have a bail hearing with the judge, and I'd likely get out on bail. It wasn't like I was a flight risk. But if they thought I murdered two women and attempted to murder another, the judge might deny bail, and I'd never sleep again.

"Rise and shine." A voice woke me from my sleep. Sun seeped in through the crack of a window above my bed. Apparently, I *would* sleep if I stayed in jail. The thought didn't make me feel much better.

The door slid open to reveal Miss Alpha. "Come on. Your attorney is here to see you."

She cuffed my hands in front of me and led me down the hall, her grip tight—too tight—on my upper arm.

"Don't think your attorney will get you out of this mess. I hear they have cold hard evidence against you."

"What is your deal?" I asked. "You were so nice at the reservoir, and now you hate me because you think I'm guilty of a crime I didn't commit?"

"I hate law-breakers," she said. "And you're even worse. You tarnished the badge."

"I'm innocent. My ex-boyfriend is setting me up," I said. "He's a tool and a half."

She yanked me forward, making me almost trip over my feet.

"Everyone says they're being set up. The judge will see right through it."

We arrived at a small room I'd never been in before.

"Rylie." A man stood when I walked in. He was short and balding, probably in his mid-fifties, wearing a suit and tie. "It's a pleasure to meet you. My name is Renaldo Martinez. Your fiancé hired me."

Miss Alpha pushed me down in the chair across the table from him.

"Was that necessary?" he asked. "I think you can treat my client with more respect."

"I don't treat murderers with respect," she said, and the walked out of the room.

"I'm sorry about that," he said. "How are you doing?"

"Not great, honestly," I said. "They found evidence in my home of a crime I didn't commit."

"Tell me about that." He opened a notebook and began scribbling notes in handwriting even a kindergarten teacher wouldn't be able to decipher.

"My ex, Troy, was in my apartment when I got home.

He planted the items there. I think he might be responsible for the attacks. Apparently, all the women were women he slept with when he and I were together."

"But you're happily engaged to someone else now, correct?"

"Yes. I have no ill feelings toward Troy other than I think he's a terrible human being."

"So some ill feelings." He gave me a sweet smile.

"Okay, some." I sighed. "But not enough to kill anyone."

"I see here they have you on attempted murder of Troy too?"

"What?" I jumped out of my chair, and the door swung open.

"Sit down," Miss Alpha shouted.

"She's fine," Renaldo said. "And I do hope you're not listening to our conversation. Attorney-client privilege and all."

She smirked and closed the door.

I sat back down. "I didn't try to kill Troy. He lunged at me. I think he lunged to get hit in the head with the baton intentionally."

"The baton you were holding?"

"I didn't know who was in my apartment. I grabbed the only two weapons I could to protect myself."

"Why didn't you simply call the police?"

"My dog was inside. I wanted to make sure he was okay." My thoughts went back to Fizzy. Surely Shayla would have gotten him out of the bathroom by now, even if she had to get our landlord—Mrs. Hudson—to help.

"Garrett was right. You're a brave woman."

"Garrett said I'm brave?" A speck of warmth lit inside me.

"Among other positive attributes."

"Look, I'll give you all the details about how it's not even possible that I hurt any of those women. I have verifiable alibis for all three."

"That would be very helpful."

"When Michelle was attacked, I just finished up talking to Nikki. Also, Ansel—who probably won't testify to anything—knows it wasn't me. He saw the person who did it. He called her the wolf lady."

He nodded and scribbled notes.

"Victoria's is a bit more convoluted. Ansel, again, was there. He was with me when she started calling out for help. I ran to the office, which Victoria had already locked and armed. I was the only person other than Victoria in the park who had a key to that office. There will be records with the alarm company that I opened that door at the same time she was calling out for help."

"And where were Victoria's keys?"

"On her belt," I said, sure I would have noticed if something was missing from her belt. I had checked, after all.

"Good. And what about the third woman?"

"Olivia," I said. "I was with a woman named Becky Frederickson when Olivia was attacked in the bathroom. I thought Becky might have been responsible for the attacks, so I was asking her questions about them. But obviously, it wasn't her since she was with me when Olivia was attacked and the sunglasses were left and her ring was stolen."

I took a breath to contain the verbal vomit.

"But they found the rings and sunglasses were found in your apartment?"

"That's what it looked like in the photographs Detective Bryant showed me."

"And you think your ex set you up because he's responsible?"

"I know for a fact he was involved with Victoria. I saw him with Olivia moments before she was attacked. And Victoria's fiancé—the one from the FBI—"

"Oh yes, I've met him."

"He said Troy and Michelle were involved too. He also said there were more women, so they might be in danger." If anything, Troy needed to be taken off the streets so that he didn't hurt anyone else.

"Is there anything else you can think of that might clear your name?"

My mind reeled. I'd been thinking about this since I'd been put into handcuffs. It was too bad Shayla and I hadn't installed cameras in our apartment.

A thought flashed through my head. "Do you think you could call Mrs. Hudson—the owner of my apartment complex?"

"I can do that. What would you like me to tell her?"

"Can you ask if she has any cameras around the apartments? Maybe even in the parking lot that might show that Troy got there before I did or something?"

"It's worth a shot," he said. "I'll see what I can do."

He stood and knocked on the door.

Miss Alpha opened it.

"I'll be seeing you soon," he said to me, then turned to her. "Be nice, or I'll have your job."

She looked panicked for a half-second, then opened her mouth to say something, but Renaldo was already gone.

"Get up," she said.

I stood and let her walk me back to my cell. This time, she didn't squeeze my arm too tightly.

25

The sky was getting dark when I heard a whisper from my door. It slid to the side, and Shayla walked in. "Let's get you out of here."

"Are you breaking me out of jail?" I whispered, my brain fuzzy with boredom.

"They're letting you go," she said. "They have proof you didn't do it."

"Proof?"

"Your attorney talked to Mrs. Hudson. Did you know she has hidden cameras down every hallway?"

I shook my head, no.

"They have video footage of Troy breaking into our apartment carrying a small bag that we believe contained the rings and sunglasses. I found the bag beneath your bed."

"So I can just go?"

"You're innocent. They have proof. They can't keep you."

I hugged her.

"But before you go, Detective Bryant wants to talk to you."

"Nope," I said. "I have nothing to say to him. He's the one—"

"Who begged to be the one to interrogate you."

"Begged?"

"He knew the whole time you were innocent. He didn't want the FBI guys jumping down your throat."

"He did a good enough job of that himself," I said.

"I'm sure it wasn't nearly as bad as it could have been." She handed me my bag of personal belongings. "Trust me, he was protecting you. And now, I think he wants your help."

"Well, isn't that a funny turn of events?"

"It is," Shayla smiled.

Once I was dressed, Shayla took me down a hallway I'd never been down before. It led to Bryant's office.

He stood from his desk when he saw me come in. "Thank you for agreeing to meet with me. I apologize for the interrogation yesterday."

"First thing's first," I said. "Have they arrested Troy?"

Bryant looked at Shayla then back at me. "Troy is missing."

"But from what Elliot said—"

Bryant frowned at the mention of Elliot.

"—there are several other women who could be next."

"Including you," Bryant said.

"I don't think Troy will hurt me," I said. "If he was, he

could have easily done it that day in my apartment. I think he wanted to frame me. He seems to be quite upset that his exes are getting engaged."

"What makes you different?" Bryant asked.

"Maybe it's something Troy said." I thought back to when we were talking in the apartment before the FBI showed up. "He told me at least I had the title of being his girlfriend. As if that made me special somehow."

"You think he's killing the women he had affairs with but wanted to frame you since you were his girlfriend?"

"Maybe he's maddest at me because he gave me the title of girlfriend and I left him. So instead of just killing me, he'd frame me for something that would send me to prison for the rest of my life." I shrugged. "I don't know. Either way, I don't think I'm a target of his violence."

"I'd feel better if we had an officer watch out for you," Bryant said.

"Shayla's with me almost all the time," I said, smiling over at my friend. "And when she's not, it's because I'm at work or Garrett's house. At work, I don't work alone anymore, and Garrett has a great security system. I'm completely safe, I promise."

Bryant was quiet for a few moments, then finally agreed. "Okay, but if we get word that Troy is anywhere near you, you'll have police all over the place."

"And here I thought you hated me." I fluttered my eyelashes for effect.

"Hate is a strong word." He smiled. "Now tell me everything you have and let's see if we can find this guy and get him behind bars."

We spent the next two hours talking about all the

possibilities. For once, I felt like a valued member of the team. Well, other than when Luke had been there.

"Should we get ice cream?" Shayla asked as we made our way home in her Volkswagen Beetle.

"Do we have any at home?" I asked. "I'd love to take a shower and get all the jail germs off me."

"I think we might have a few pints in the freezer," Shayla said. "I'm sorry they arrested you."

"It's okay," I said. "I'm sure it looked pretty bad, evidence wise."

"Yeah, but still." She knew it looked bad, but she also knew me and knew that I hadn't hurt anyone.

"You know, I forgot to admit to the one thing I did do."

"Don't admit anything to me. I have a duty—"

"I dropped my baton on Troy's balls."

Shayla's eyes widened, then she burst out laughing. "Good. He deserved it."

I laughed too. "The cops told me to drop my weapons. It just so happened his junk was right below my baton." I shrugged.

"Do you think they'll find him?" Shayla asked.

"I don't know," I said. "He's smart. He knows how to talk his way out of things, and he's a trained cop."

She parked the car in an available space right next to Cherry Anne, and we headed up to the apartment.

When she unlocked the door, we both stood in shock.

Troy was sitting on our couch, drinking a beer.

"What's up, ladies?" He was drunk. Beer bottles surrounded him. He had to have drunk every single one in our fridge. So much for being smart.

Shayla picked up her phone and dialed 9-1-1.

Fizzy barked from the bathroom.

"No, please don't call the police. They want to arrest me." Troy let out a hiccup and then laughed, almost falling off the couch.

"Of course, they want to arrest you," I said as Shayla spoke softly into the phone. "You killed two women, and another one is hanging on by a thread."

"I didn't do it," he said.

"Then how did you get their rings?" I desperately wanted to free Fizzy, but I kept my distance and stood in the doorway in case Troy tried something stupid.

"Those pieces of shit?" He laughed again. "Those women didn't deserve those rings. They were horrible human beings. They cheated on you."

"No, they didn't cheat on me," I said. "You did."

He waved a hand in the air as if it was the same thing.

"At least I loved you," he said. "I never loved them."

"I think the only person you love is yourself," I said.

"I have a girlfriend, you know."

"That's great." I peeked back at Shayla, who was still speaking to the police. "I hope she enjoys visiting you in jail."

Anger replaced the laughter on his face. "I'm not going to jail. I told you I didn't do anything wrong. Plus, I'm a cop, you're just some lowly park ranger. They won't believe you over me."

"If they believed you, do you think I'd be out of jail right now?" I asked. "They have evidence against you."

"What evidence?" He narrowed his eyes at me.

"Video evidence," I said. "And probably fingerprint evidence."

"I wore gloves."

"I bet you did," I replied, shocked he'd admitted to the crimes. "Why did you do it?"

"Because I wanted you to go to jail. You left me and found some big-shot accountant who doesn't deserve you."

"You cheated on me," I said. "Multiple times. Probably more times than you can count."

"Forty-seven."

Ugh. What a jerk.

"Why are you here?"

"To win you back." He tipped his head back and laughed. "Just kidding. I'd never want to be with you again."

"There's one thing we can agree on then."

He stopped laughing, grabbed a beer bottle, and chucked it at me.

I ducked just in time, and the bottle smashed on the door across the hallway.

"What the hell?" Shayla asked. "Stop provoking him."

It was too late. He was throwing more bottles. I stayed out of sight and hoped our neighbor across the hall didn't open their door.

"Are the cops almost here?" I asked.

Sirens answered my question.

"You called the cops?" Troy screamed from inside the apartment, bottles still shattering inside—his aim seemingly getting worse.

"Five minutes," Bryant said when he topped the stairs with several other cops behind him. "You haven't been alone five minutes, and you're already in danger. *Now* do you want an officer around?"

"Won't need one." A bottle broke on the door frame next to me. "As long as your guys can get him in cuffs."

"Go," he said, and the officers dressed in helmets, face shields, and bullet-proof vests entered the apartment.

"Put the bottles down," they ordered.

"Oh, come on," Troy said. "I was just playing. I'm an officer too."

"Troy Shipley, you're under arrest."

"Don't touch me." It sounded like Troy was struggling. "I didn't hurt those women. You can't prove anything. I wore gloves. I was just trying to protect her."

"Trying to protect me from what?" I whispered to Shayla.

She shrugged. "What does he mean he wore gloves?"

"Sounds like an admission of guilt to me," I said.

"I guess we got our man," Bryant said. "Thanks for your help on the case."

I nodded, surprised he was thanking me when only months before he had me fired and nearly thrown in jail for investigating.

When they pulled Troy out of my apartment, he sneered at me. "You'll regret not coming back to me. Mark my words. That guy you're *engaged* to is a dud."

"Thankfully, your opinion doesn't matter to me," I said. "Oh, and I forgive you."

"*You* forgive *me*?" Troy's voice was climbing in pitch. "I didn't do anything wrong. I don't accept your forgiveness."

"Thankfully, forgiveness is not for the forgiven but for the forgiver."

Shayla beamed at me.

"Let's go," Bryant said.

"A dud, huh?" Garrett's voice came from the stairway.

"Just calling it like I see it," Troy said. "She'll get bored with you. Won't take much."

"I guess we'll just have to wait and see, won't we?" Garrett let them pass and then gathered me up into his arms. "I'm so glad you're okay."

"Me too," I said. "And you're not a dud. I won't get bored with you."

"I know," he said.

"I love you."

"I love you too," he said. "Now, let's get Fizzy out of that bathroom, poor guy."

26

My ring was back on my hand, sparkling proudly when I returned to work.

"Sorry, you had to cover for me," I told Ben when I saw him at the shop.

"It wasn't a problem." He lowered his voice. "I got a day to myself. Not that Tatiana isn't great, she just really likes to talk."

"I hear she has some great stories, though."

"Yeah," he said. "It sounds like being a ranger in Florida is much more exciting than here. At least when it comes to wildlife."

"There you are," Ursula said from behind me.

I turned, and before I could react, she had me in a huge bear hug.

"Thank you so much for finding the man responsible for Victoria's attack."

"I didn't do much," I said. "I'm still in shock that Troy would do something like that. I mean, he's a pompous jerk, but I didn't think he had it in him to hurt people like that."

"Didn't he throw a bunch of beer bottles at you?" Ben asked. Word traveled fast in our workgroup. My guess was Shayla told Seamus, who told Dusty, who told Ben.

"He was wasted," I said.

"You're a hero," Ursula said. "And Victoria woke up today."

"Wait, she did?" I asked.

Ursula nodded but looked sad.

"That's good news, right?" I said.

"She doesn't remember what happened," Ursula replied.

"About the attack?" Ben asked.

Ursula shook her head. "She remembers Ansel freaking out on her, but that's it."

"So, she can't testify against Troy," I said.

Ursula shook her head.

"I think they have enough evidence against him anyway." I was trying to reassure her, but even I didn't know if a jury would convict him beyond a reasonable doubt.

"What if they don't?" Ben asked.

"He goes free and who knows what he'll do," Ursula said. "But let's try not to think that way. I want to believe our justice system will prevail this time."

"I'm just glad Victoria is okay," I said. "Do you think I could come by after my shift and visit her?"

"I don't know why you'd want to after the way she behaved and what Elliot did."

I shrugged. "She once asked if she and I could be friends. I guess I want to see if that might still be a possibility." My words surprised everyone, including me. "A friend reminded me that Victoria did me a favor. And knowing now that Troy is not only a cheating piece of dog poo, he also has a violent nature. She did me a double favor."

"I'm glad we have you, Rylie," Ursula said. "I'm sure Victoria would love to see you."

Ursula said her goodbyes after thanking me about a dozen more times, and Ben went home, leaving me alone in the park.

Even though I knew Troy was locked up, it felt strange being here alone. Greg was at Shadow Trail Reservoir, not too far away, and Seamus was out on the trails in the city, so I wasn't truly alone, but still.

Nevertheless, the shift passed by quickly without incident.

As I was finishing my closing procedure, I saw a familiar figure running down the trail.

Naked guy.

I laughed to myself.

"What are you doing here so late?" I asked when our paths crossed. I kept my eyes focused on his face.

"Ah sorry," he said. "I know I should be out of the park by now, but I've enjoyed running after hours. I guess if you need to give me a ticket, go ahead."

"You know you were supposed to be out of the gates a half hour ago."

"The reservoir is just so peaceful this time of night."

"How do you get in and out?" I tried not to picture

him climbing over the fence naked. It couldn't be comfortable.

"Some of the fence is pretty low in places." He shrugged. "I did hurdles in high school."

Made sense. "Just head out the nearest gate, okay? I can't officially leave you in the park alone, so I'll wait until you're out."

"Will do," he said. "And thanks."

"Next time, I might not be so forgiving."

"Noted." He smiled and took off at a sprint toward the gate. He'd be out in less than five minutes.

Once I saw him expertly jump the fence—not that I was watching or anything—I headed to the shop and switched the ranger truck for Cherry Anne, locked the main gate, and headed to the hospital.

———

Victoria was sitting up in bed when I walked in. Elliot was not in the room, nor were her mom or aunt.

"Hey," I said.

She looked shy. "Hi."

"I'm happy you're okay."

"I'm so sorry." Tears welled up in her eyes. "I should never have slept with that dirtbag. I knew he was with you, and I was with Elliot, but I did and it was stupid and it almost got me killed."

"Do you remember him attacking you?"

She slowly shook her head. "No. I don't remember anything after talking to Ansel."

"You should see Ansel now," I said. "He shaved his

head and is a completely different person.”

"I know,” she said. “He came to visit me earlier today.”

This surprised me. “Really?”

"Yeah,” she said. “He looked different, but he was still the same old Ansel.”

"So he was high?”

"Have you ever seen him not high?”

"When I first saw him with a shaved head, he wasn't high,” I said. “The board of his company gave him an ultimatum and said he had to stay sober because he was losing his short-term memory.”

"His memory seemed to be fine when he was here. We talked all about that night. He said you ran to save me when you heard me screaming over the radio.”

"Did he say anything else?” I asked. “Like did he see anything?”

"He swears up and down it was wolf lady, but I told him it was Troy.” She readjusted herself in bed. “I would have shown him a picture, but Troy changed his social media profile.”

My mind reeled. If only I would have been able to talk to Ansel when he was high.

"How long ago was he here?” I asked.

"A few hours,” she said. “He said he had to get sobered up before a big meeting tonight. Hopefully, they're not firing him.”

"Maybe he'll be back at the reservoir tomorrow,” I said. “I should probably let you get some rest.”

"Do you think you can ever forgive me?” Her voice was small.

"You're already forgiven, my friend.”

Her face widened into a smile. "Thanks, Rylie."

27

I could hardly wait to get to work hoping I could talk to Ansel. I found an old picture of Troy that I stuffed in my pocket so I could show him. Maybe Troy had dressed up as a werewolf to blend in at the event. That way, I wouldn't recognize him.

On my way, my phone rang. It was my mom.

"Hello?"

"What is this I hear about you being arrested for murder?"

Right to the point.

"It was a mix-up."

"Obviously." Mom sounded exasperated. "And now I hear they have Troy locked up."

"Apparently, he had some mental health issues I wasn't aware of."

"That's unfortunate," she said. "But what's really unfortunate is that you wasted such a big part of your life on him. I told you to stay with Luke, but nooooo."

I took a breath. "But now I have Garrett."

"And you better not mess that up."

I laughed.

"How's the wedding planning?"

"We have a venue," I said. I'd already texted her with the date. "The Big Mountain Lodge and Resort."

My mom squealed on the other end. "I love that place. What a great idea. I'll get the payment sent right over."

"Garrett wanted to help with it if you're okay with that."

"Absolutely not," Mom said, as I'd suspected she would. "You two save your money for your life together. If he put down a deposit, I'll make sure the lodge refunds it directly to him."

"Thanks," I said.

"When are we going dress shopping?"

"I'll have to look at my schedule. And maybe start running more. I'd like to lose a few pounds before—"

"You don't need to lose a single ounce. I'll talk to your sister, and we'll figure out a time."

"Sounds good."

"Okay, I have to go make your father lunch. Love you."

"Love you too, Mom."

I hung up and smiled. It was exciting thinking about the wedding. I thought about wedding dresses until I pulled up to the shop.

"The park is quiet today," Antonio said when we met for shift change. "You shouldn't have any issues."

"Thanks," I said.

"I am glad you're not in danger anymore . . . or jail."

"Me too." I laughed. "How are things with Sondra?"

"Same. It might be a long summer."

"That's for sure. Victoria woke up."

"Did she remember Troy attacking her?"

"No. Forgot the whole incident."

"Too bad. Hopefully, they have enough to convict him without her statement."

I shrugged. I didn't want to think about it. The sun was out, there was a gentle breeze cooling the air, and everything was great.

"Have a good day," Antonio finally said before straddling his Ducati.

I'd be lying if I said I didn't notice how incredibly attractive he was in that moment.

That was my fatal flaw—attraction to the bad boy.

I chose Troy over Luke.

I wasn't about to choose another bad boy—even if this one wasn't a complete psychopath—over the steady and wonderful guy I had.

The day was perfect. The fishermen were happy because the fish were biting, the joggers sang along to the music coming from their headphones, and the three adorable kids on the beach built the perfect sandcastle.

"Any news on the summies?" Carmen said behind me as I stood overlooking the beach.

"You really shouldn't sneak up on people," I said. "And no. They seem to be up to their usual non-sharing selves."

"Why do you think Ursula really hired them?"

"Who knows? But if it was to make sure I wasn't

investigating anything, she shot herself in the foot when she asked me to investigate."

"Wouldn't she have just let them go and found replacements?"

"They've all already been through training," I said. "It would be silly to go through that all over again with a new round of them."

"They creep me out." Carmen wrapped her arms around herself. "The old guy—"

"George."

"—if that is his real name."

I laughed.

"*George* is the worst of all of them. Sometimes I think he's watching me."

"Maybe he thinks you're cute."

"Or maybe he thinks I'm up to something."

"Are you?"

Carmen raised an eyebrow.

"Never mind, I don't want to know."

She looked out at the beach. "I'm taking off. You good?"

"Yep," I said. "Only a few more hours and I'll be on my way home."

She turned toward the office.

"Oh, and have you heard anything about Ansel being back?"

"The stoner from the playground?"

I nodded.

"Nope."

"Okay, thanks." I couldn't help being disappointed. I'd

hoped he would have had some sort of information for me.

The next couple of hours drug on and on. I checked my phone every five minutes, hoping an hour had magically passed.

I was rounding the top of the dam when my phone vibrated with a text message. Then it vibrated again. And again.

I stopped the truck and pulled up the texts.

The first one was from Shayla.

Another woman was beaten. Missing ring, aviator glasses.

My stomach soured. The second was from Bryant.

Where are you?

The third was from Jerry.

They're letting Troy out. Just thought you should know.

I typed a response to Shayla.

Is she connected to Troy?

Then Bryant.

Working at Alder Ridge.

Then Jerry.

Thanks for the heads up.

Bryant responded first.

Don't leave. Stay somewhere safe. If the FBI tries to arrest you, have them call me first.

Great, the FBI thought it was me again? I'd been at work all day.

Shayla's response came back seconds later.

Yes. Another one of his escapades. Be careful.

I was about to type my response to Shayla when something hit my window. I dropped my phone between the seat and the center console and grabbed for my pepper spray.

The top of the dam wasn't well-lit, but the moon was bright.

Thankfully, it was only naked guy.

I put my pepper spray back and rolled down my window.

"I'm glad you didn't spray me with that, it probably would have hurt my man parts."

"I don't usually aim for the man parts," I said. "What's up."

"Just wanted to let you know I'd be out of the park on time tonight."

"That's progress," I said. "Any chance your next step would be clothes?"

He laughed. "Unlikely."

It was worth a shot. "Hey, before you go." A thought popped into my mind. "You said you've been running late every night. Do you ever run down by the office?"

"Sometimes," he said. "I like to keep my route varied, though."

"About a week ago, one of the rangers was attacked in the banquet hall."

He nodded. "I remember seeing the cops and hiding in the bushes. They don't take as kindly to my free style of running as you rangers do."

"I bet not," I said. "Anyway, do you remember seeing anyone else that night? Anyone who wasn't a cop or medic or me?"

"I saw that guy who hides underneath the slide. He's creepy if you ask me."

"Ansel?"

"I guess." He shrugged. "Took off running the other way."

"Anyone else?"

"Just Hilary," he said.

"Hilary?"

"You know the one who looks like you, only scarier. The one with the dogs?"

The jailer—Miss Alpha? I hadn't seen her that night. And I hadn't known her name was Hilary.

Then it felt like my brain felt like it exploded. Ansel had been telling the truth, in a way. She wasn't a wolf, but she was queen of the wolves. She directed the dogs as if she was their queen.

"Did she seem suspicious at all?"

"Well, she didn't have her dogs with her, if that's what you're asking. And she ran out the gate instead of to her car, which she usually parks in the parking lot."

This guy had excellent observation skills.

"Do you know where she was running from?"

"I think the beach or something. She was pretty sneaky. Do you think she had something to do with the attack?"

"I think it's entirely possible."

He started jogging away. "Good luck with that. I hope she doesn't strike again."

My heart raced in my chest.

I reached between the seats to try to get my phone, but it was no use, it was too far down.

I'd have to get out of the truck to get it, but if I did and Hilary was around, I might be the next target.

I decided I'd be safer in the office than in the truck.

I drove down the sidewalk and parked right next to the office. That way, I could get in my truck fast if I needed to.

I checked my surroundings four times before I hopped out of the truck, reached down between the seats, snatched my phone, and ran to the office door.

I fumbled for the right key, kicking myself that I hadn't been prepared with it before I'd gotten out of the truck.

"You look panicked," a quiet voice said from behind me. I dropped the keys and turned to find Hilary ten feet away, holding a baton just like mine.

"Do I need to be panicked?" I asked.

"Oh probably." She took a step toward me.

I pushed the red button on the mic on my shoulder. "This is Rylie Cooper at Alder Ridge Reservoir by the park office. Hilary—the jailer—is about to kill me."

I knew the line would stay open for thirty seconds, but that was all they needed to know.

"That was stupid," Hilary said.

"You won't get away with it this time," I said.

"I wasn't going to get away with it either way."

"You seemed perfectly content letting your boyfriend take the fall for you. If you hadn't attacked another woman, they never would have known it was you."

"Ex-boyfriend," she corrected. "He rolled over on me like a puppy who wanted a belly rub. And after all the work he did to try to frame you."

His words repeated in my head. When he said he was trying to protect her, he meant Hilary, not me.

Just another twist of the knife.

"They'll never get here in time," Hilary said. "Even if they dispatched a car the minute you hit the button, it would take at least ten minutes. I suspect you have about two."

When she lifted her baton, I yanked mine from my holster and extended it.

"Ooh, I like a fair fight," Hilary said. It was then that I noticed something sparkle on her head. Sparkly bobby pins had been pushed into the braid that surrounded the top of her head—a crown. The bobby pins were probably what was sparkling in the bottom of her purse that night —the reason she jerked her purse out of my sight. And with them in her braid, it could have easily been what Ansel would mistake as a crown.

"Why did you do it?"

"To warn Troy to never cheat on me." She frowned. "But he didn't get the message. I gave him three options for rings—rings that those girls didn't deserve, the little whores—but he still didn't propose."

Her eyes flickered to the ring on the hand I had raised to protect my face like Antonio had shown me. "Maybe if I had that one, he'd propose."

She swung her arm down in one fluid motion—obviously more skilled with the baton than me—but I managed to meet it with my own before it hit me square in the head.

"Ooh, it's kind of like we're sword fighting." She swung the baton again, this time aiming for my legs.

I jumped back, and when her baton swung past me, I hit her in her upper leg and waited for her to fall.

She didn't fall.

"Damnit, that hurts," she said. "I wondered what it would feel like to get hit with one myself."

I swung again, but she met my baton with hers.

"Ranger One, Ranger Seven?" My mic must have freed up from the thirty-second emergency lock. But I couldn't get distracted, and I definitely couldn't respond.

"Ranger One, Ranger Seven status?" Greg called out again.

"Go ahead, tell him you're about to die." Hilary cackled.

I clicked the mic. "I need assistance by the office now."

"Copy. Help is on the way."

I only hoped it'd get there fast enough.

"Why the glasses?" I asked, trying to get her mind off fighting.

I didn't want to kill her, didn't even want to hurt her badly, but I also didn't want to die.

"Cute touch, huh?"

I'd probably never look at aviator glasses the same way again.

"Troy wears them all the time. I thought it'd be a nice parting gift for them from the man they cheated with."

She was downright nuts.

I swung again, this time hitting her in her clavicle. But she swung at the same time and got me in the arm I'd held up to protect my face.

I felt the bones shatter—a lightning bolt of pain shooting up into my shoulder.

She'd hit me harder than I'd hit her.

She wanted to kill me. I was just trying to stay alive.

Now I had a broken arm, and she was still moving around like she hadn't felt a thing. Maybe she hadn't. Maybe she was on drugs.

I prayed the police would get there soon.

"I thought you hated law-breakers." I ground my teeth against the pain. "Aren't you tarnishing the badge doing this?"

"This is justice served in its purest form," she said. "Plus, I'll never wear a badge again. Troy decided that for me."

I almost explained to her how people were responsible for their actions but thought better of it.

I took another step back, but I was out of room, My

back was to the railing of the balcony overlooking the beach. If I jumped, I'd likely break a leg too.

"Looks like your time is up," Hilary said, her voice evil.

"For what it's worth, I'm sorry Troy was such an asshat." I was trying to distract her. Catch her off guard. "No one deserves to be cheated on or led on."

"Don't talk about my boyfriend like that." She swung and hit my broken arm again.

Pain shot from my wrist up to my neck, nearly bringing me to my knees. I could barely see through the tears in my eyes.

"Troy loved me more than he ever loved you. He told me so."

"I'm sure he did," I said. "Love you," I added quickly. "More than me." The pain was making it hard to talk. "Maybe he didn't cheat on you."

"He did," she said.

"So why didn't you go after that woman?" I considered leaping over the rail. At least then I'd be alive. "Why go after the women he cheated on me with?"

"I was just making my way through the list."

She swung again, but this time I caught her baton with my own. I spun it around like I'd seen people do in fencing.

"Cute trick." She yanked her baton away and brought it down hard across my shin.

I dropped my baton and fell to the ground, my arm cracking further under my weight.

"You know, I thought it would be more satisfying seeing you laying there ready to die." She walked toward me like a lion stalking its prey. "But I didn't expect you to put up a fight. None of the others did."

I waited until she got within inches from me, her baton raised like a sword, then I took a play from my nephew's playbook.

I swiped my good leg out as hard as I could, catching her feet and bringing her crashing down next to me.

I pulled the pepper spray from my belt and shot her directly in the face.

Thankfully, she wasn't immune to the burning sensation.

She dropped her baton and fell to her knees in agony.

I kicked the baton away from her and scooted as far away as I could in case she was also carrying a gun.

"What the hell?" she screamed. "That's not fair."

"What's not fair is you taking your jealousies out on women who don't deserve it. Troy's not worth it." My arm hurt so bad, I felt dizzy.

Thankfully, three police officers came around the corner at that moment and rushed to us.

"I'm Rylie," Hilary said. "Save me. She's trying to kill me!"

The police hesitated.

"She's lying," I said, trying to stay conscious. "I'm the park ranger, see?" I motioned to my uniform.

"She took my uniform and put it on. We're the same size. That's why Troy loved us both. We're practically twins."

"Other than she's crazy, and I'm sane," I said.

Unfortunately, none of the officers looked even remotely recognizable.

"Shayla is my best friend," Hilary said. "We live together. I have a dog named Fuzzy."

"Fizzy," I corrected. "His name is Fizzy."

"And she's trying to kill me," Hilary continued.

"Please lower your weapon," one of the officers said.

I realized I was still holding the can of pepper spray. I rolled it toward him.

"We have to arrest you both until we get this sorted," the officer said.

"My arm is broken," I said.

"She's just saying that so you won't cuff her," Hilary said. "She's dangerous."

I held up my arm, my hand and wrist jutting off at an unnatural angle.

Two of the officers looked away. It *was* pretty gross.

"Okay, I won't cuff you."

"Don't cuff me either," Hilary said. "My arm is broken too."

I sighed. This was getting ridiculous.

"Have any of you been to the Prairie City Detention Center?"

They nodded.

"She works there. Her name is Hilary something. One of you has to recognize her."

One of the officers turned on his flashlight and pointed it at her red and puffy face. She looked nothing like she usually did.

"She's telling the truth." Finally, a voice I knew. Detective Bryant came to stand next to me. "This is Rylie Cooper. That is Hilary Wentworth. Arrest that one."

They nodded and did as they were asked.

"Troy's the one who tried to frame Rylie," Hilary said, instantly throwing Troy under the bus.

"We are well aware," Bryant said. "The two of you will be locked up for a very long time."

"It was worth it," Hilary said under her breath as they walked her past me.

"Now, let's get you some medical attention," Bryant said.

They set my arm and sent me home in a cast. Garrett, Shayla, and my mom were with me the entire time—none of them wanting to leave my side even though I told them a hundred times I wasn't in danger anymore.

After taking a slightly awkward shower with my arm in a plastic bag, I decided to lay down for a nap. Fizzy snuggled up next to me—he hadn't left my side since I'd gotten home. He even went into the bathroom with me while I'd taken a shower.

I was just about to doze off when my phone rang with an unknown number.

I almost didn't answer it, but then did at the last minute.

"Hello?"

"Rylie?" The voice on the other end sounded like it was coming from the end of a tunnel. "Can you hear me?"

"Barely," I said.

"It's Luke."

I almost dropped the phone.

"Are you there?"

"Yeah," I said.

"Are you okay? Jerry emailed me about what happened."

"I'm okay," I said. "My arm is in a cast, and my leg hurts, but I'm alive."

"I wish I was there. Maybe I could have protected you."

I wanted to scream at him. Tell him he should be here.

But he'd made his decision.

And I'd made mine.

"Are you coming home for Thanksgiving?" I asked.

"Probably Christmas," he said. "I hear you'll be married by then."

"Yep, that's the plan," I said.

"Big Mountain Lodge and Resort, huh?"

"Uh, yeah," I hated telling him that knowing it could have been where we would have gotten married if I'd accepted his proposal all those years ago.

"I'm sure it'll be a beautiful wedding."

"Thanks. How are you doing?"

"Good," he said. "The work over here is great. I feel like I'm making a difference."

"I'm glad you're enjoying yourself." I don't know why tears stung at the corners of my eyes. Maybe the old saying was right. You never got over your first true love. Or perhaps I was just exhausted, and the pain meds were getting to me.

"I better go, this call is probably costing us both a fortune."

I didn't care. I didn't want to stop talking yet.

"I guess I just wanted to hear your voice and make sure you were okay," he said.

"I'm okay," I said.

"Good." I could hear a small smile in his voice. "Take care."

"You too."

The line disconnected.

I wrapped my good arm around Fizzy's neck and let the tears fall down my cheeks.

When I woke up, people filled my apartment. Shayla had cooked up a meal and invited practically everyone I knew. The rangers, Victoria and Ursula, my family, Garrett, Bella, Brock, and Boyd, Logan, Eli, and Mrs. Hudson, and even Jerry and Detective Bryant.

They cheered when I walked out.

Joy flooded through me. I pushed away my sadness about Luke and focused on the here and now.

I gave almost everyone hugs as they told me how thankful they were I was okay.

When I approached my family, my sword-wielding nephew came up and hugged me. "You beat the bad guy?"

"I hope you don't mind. I used one of your techniques."

His face lit up. "Really?"

"The leg kick-out," I said. "Worked like a charm."

He hugged me more tightly.

"You'll make a great mom someday," Garrett whispered in my ear.

"Thank you." I kissed him and made my way over to the food. "This looks amazing, Shay."

Shayla shuffled closer. "I hear you talked to Luke."

I looked around to make sure Garrett was out of earshot, not that he would care since Luke was in a different country and all, but still.

"He was just checking in."

"Does he sound okay?"

"Haven't you talked to him?"

"He hasn't called me," she said. "From what I know, he hasn't called anyone. He's emailed Jerry and me a couple of times, but that's it."

"I guess getting your arm broken comes with its benefits." I held up my cast and laughed.

"Speaking of, I need to break that pinky of yours."

She reached for my good hand, but I yanked it away.

"Come on," she said. "You pinky promised you would be extra super careful."

"I tried!"

She laughed. "I guess I can let you off the hook on this one since your entire arm is broken, but next time I won't be so forgiving."

She wrapped an arm around my shoulders giving me a side-hug.

"Who's ready to shop for wedding dresses?" My mom approached with my sister in tow. "I know you said to wait, but I made an appointment for later today. I figured with your arm like that you probably couldn't work."

"But who will train me?" Victoria asked from behind us. "Sorry, I didn't mean to eavesdrop, but . . ."

"Rylie can still work. And train you," Ursula said. "As long as she feels up to it."

"Yes," I said, almost too quickly.

"You're a glutton for punishment," Mom said. "But I'm proud of you. Now, are we good to go dress shopping this afternoon?"

"I wish I were going dress shopping," Victoria said, holding up her hand. "I broke it off with Elliot. After what he did to you, I just couldn't stay with him."

I wrapped an arm around her shoulder. "You can do better than him."

"You think?"

"I know," I said. "If it isn't too sad for you, you can come with us to look at dresses."

Victoria's face lit up. "I'd love that."

I turned and caught sight of my sister, Megan. "Hey, can I talk to you?"

She nodded and followed me into the kitchen.

"I haven't had a chance to ask because everything has been so crazy, but will you be my maid of honor?"

Her face lit up, and tears sprung to her eyes. "Really?"

"You're my sister. My best friend since birth. Who else would I choose?"

She hugged me so tight, I thought my cast might pop off. It was a good thing I was on some good pain killers.

"One more question," I asked when she finally let me go.

"Shoot."

"How did you know Tom was the one?"

She paused for a minute and thought.

"There was this moment," she said. "Right before I fell asleep one night when I heard him whisper that he loved me more than anything in the entire world. And I realized I loved him more than literally anything in the entire world too."

I looked over my shoulder at Garrett. Did I love him more than anything in the entire world?

"Is everything okay with you and Garrett?"

I turned back to her with the sincerest smile I could muster. "Everything is perfect."

Thank you so much for reading *Whacked*!

I would be honored and eternally grateful if you would post a review on Amazon and/or Goodreads about the book.

Also, I love hearing from readers! Email me at stellabixbyauthor@gmail.com.

XOXO,

Stella Bixby

ACKNOWLEDGMENTS

Books can be so hard to write and even harder to share with others.

This book was no different. It was a challenge, but so many people in my life made it more bearable.

As always, I thank God first and foremost, and my family as a close second.

My beta readers are so incredibly important. They help me polish each book until it shines. Thank you all for your help.

To my ARC team, you are the best! I am always so excited to share my newest creation with you!

And last but never ever least, thank you to every single person who reads this book. I hope you like it!

ABOUT THE AUTHOR

Stella Bixby is a native Coloradan who loves to snow-board, pluck at the guitar, and play board games with her family. She was once a volunteer firefighter and a park ranger, but now spends most of her time making up stories and trying to figure out what to cook for dinner.

Connect with Stella on Facebook, Twitter, and Instagram @StellaBixby.

Stella loves to hear from her readers!
www.stellabixby.com

www.ingramcontent.com/pod-product-compliance
Lightning Source LLC
Chambersburg PA
CBHW021141190726
48288CB00008B/2765